PUFFIN BOOKS

The Racehorse
Who Wouldn't Gallop

CLARE BALDING

The Racehorse Who Wouldn't Gallop

Illustrated by TONY ROSS

PUFFIN

PUFFIN BOOKS

UK | USA | Canada | Ireland | Australia
India | New Zealand | South Africa

Puffin Books is part of the Penguin Random House group of companies
whose addresses can be found at global.penguinrandomhouse.com.

www.penguin.co.uk
www.puffin.co.uk
www.ladybird.co.uk

Penguin
Random House
UK

First published 2016

001

Text copyright © Clare Balding, 2016
Illustrations copyright © Tony Ross, 2016

The moral right of the author and illustrator has been asserted

Set in 12.25/20 AbsaraOT
Typeset by Jouve (UK) Milton Keynes
Printed in Great Britain by Clays Ltd, St Ives plc

A CIP catalogue record for this book is available from the British Library

ISBN: 978-0-141-36290-8

All correspondence to:
Puffin Books
Penguin Random House Children's
80 Strand, London WC2R 0RL

For Jonno, Toby and Flora

The Folly Farm family

Charlie

Mrs Bass

Mr Bass

Harry

Larry

Joe

Chapter 1

Chapter 1

Charlie Bass woke early, partly because her window didn't have any curtains and partly because Boris the Border terrier was licking her face.

Boris wasn't technically allowed to sleep on Charlie's bed. He spent every evening curled up neatly on an old blanket in the corner of her room, not far from the saucepan that collected the drips that found their way through the roof when it rained. But every night, as her mother closed the door after kissing Charlie goodnight, Boris slipped off the blanket, silently jumped up on to the bed and curled neatly into the curve of Charlie's body where he stayed until it was time to give Charlie her morning wash.

'Boris, get off!' said Charlie, playfully pushing his head away.

Boris just wagged his tail as if she'd said, 'Oh, Boris, you *are* brilliant!'

Sitting up in bed, Charlie stared out of the window, trying to remember the details of her dream. She had been riding again, so fast it had made her eyes stream. In the clouds, she imagined she could see the shapes of horses, a whole herd of wild grey ponies from the Camargue, galloping on a beach in France.

The walls of Charlie's bedroom were papered with posters of horses: the Olympic gold-medal-winning dressage horse Valegro dancing on the spot, the showjumper Hello Sanctos clearing an impossibly high wall and a big grey event horse stretching over the Vicarage Vee at Badminton.

Above her rickety chest of drawers (which had a couple of knobs missing and one stuck on with chewing gum) was a picture of a palomino pony from a calendar she had been given for Christmas two years earlier. Charlie didn't know its name or where it came from, but she looked at it every day and imagined owning a pony like that. A pony she could call her own. A pony she could build a partnership and a relationship with. A pony only she would understand and who, given time, would understand her too.

Charlie knew that she could be a top-class rider if she was given the chance, but so far she had only ever ridden a cow. Her dad told her it was the same thing, but she knew that it wasn't. Charlie couldn't imagine a life that wasn't surrounded by cows and chickens and pigs and large muddy fields. Her family lived on a farm at the end of a long and bumpy drive in the middle of nowhere. They were five miles from the nearest village, twenty miles from the nearest town and it was so dark at night that the stars were bright and clear.

Boris licked her again and Charlie ruffled his head, sniffing. He had clearly been rolling in the muck heap again.

'Come on, Boris, you stinky boy, let's get going,' she said. 'We've got eggs to find and pigs to feed.'

Charlie had been christened Charlotte Elizabeth Bass, but her father thought that sounded a bit formal, so had called her Charlie from day one. Along with her older brothers, Harry and Larry, Charlie worked on the farm before and after she went to school.

Charlie's mother Caroline was copy-editor for a major publishing firm. It meant that she read the first drafts of non-fiction books, checking them for spelling, grammar and factual errors. She read at least a book a day, sometimes two, and was a mine of information on subjects from bee-keeping to Buddhism, trees to trampolines, ancient mythology to modern art.

She had fallen in love with Charlie's dad, Bill Bass, at the Three Counties Show, where he was showing a cow. It didn't win the main prize (in fact, it came last), but, when Charlie's mum went to commiserate with him afterwards, she was bowled over by his charm.

'I realized it was your dad who should've won first prize. He was gorgeous,' Charlie's mum had told her once.

Charlie's dad worked every hour that the sun was up – and some hours when it wasn't. He milked the cows at 5 a.m. and again at 5 p.m. every day of the year. They had to be milked in a particular order because cows are very keen on routine and all have individual personalities and quirks. Bill liked to talk to them as he attached them to the milking machine, addressing them by their names. He had chosen simple, easy-to-remember names, while his wife had called several after characters from books. Charlie and her brothers had thrown in a few celebrities for good measure, which meant that the herd was quite a mix . . .

So Princess Anne was milked first every morning, followed by Windy Bottom, Creamy and Hermione

Granger. Madonna waited patiently for her turn towards the end, while Jane Eyre and Moll Flanders always produced huge quantities of milk.

Harry and Larry were supposed to help out with the milking, but they weren't very good, so Mrs Bass had persuaded her husband to employ a teenager called Joe. He had come to the area when his father, a well-known jockey, had died after a bad fall. The Basses had welcomed him with open arms, and they soon discovered Joe was a very hard worker. He had quickly become like one of the family.

Charlie spotted him through the kitchen window as he stepped out of the milking shed for a breath of fresh air, and hurried over to him with a cup of tea.

'Oh, that's just what I need. Thanks, Charlie,' said Joe. He seemed relieved to see her.

Charlie slipped her arms round his waist and gave him a hug.

'Joe . . . I know it's the anniversary of your dad's accident today. Mum says to tell you that she's made your favourite breakfast and you're to come in as soon as the milking's finished.'

Joe looked down at Charlie and blinked hard. She knew what to say and exactly how to say it.

'Thanks, Charlie, and say thanks to your mum too. We'll be there in ten minutes. We've only got Nancy Drew and Taylor Swift left to do.'

'So what was the best horse you ever saw?' asked Charlie as the family tucked into a full English breakfast at the kitchen table. Her mum wasn't the best cook, but what she lacked in technique she made up for with enthusiasm.

'Well, it was when my dad was working in Newmarket,' replied Joe, carefully cutting off the burnt bits from his sausage. 'There was a horse called Lightning Bolt who was so fast they had to use two other horses to stay with him on the gallops. One to lead him for the first half and another one to jump in halfway and lead him for the last four furlongs because nothing was quick enough to stay with him for the whole mile.'

Charlie loved to talk about horses with Joe. He hadn't ridden since his dad had died, but he had lived close to the huge yard in Newmarket where his father had been Head Lad, the trainer's second in command.

After incessant begging, Joe had helped Charlie learn to ride on a very forgiving dairy cow called Ermintrude. It's not easy to ride a cow, particularly without a saddle or a bridle, but Charlie had natural balance and strong legs so she could stay on for hours. Joe was impressed.

'Right, that's enough about horses,' said Charlie's mum. 'Time for school.'

'*Muuum*,' moaned Charlie. 'Do I have to go?'

'You need a proper education,' Mrs Bass replied as she poured fresh milk into a chipped mug and pushed it across the kitchen table.

'What for? There aren't any exams that will help me do what I want to do.'

'Even professional riders have passed their exams,' said Mrs Bass. 'And, if you get good grades, we could see about finding you a pony to ride.'

Charlie grinned. 'All right then.'

This wasn't the first time her mum had mentioned getting a pony, and the vague promise was normally enough to get Charlie to school. But deep down she knew that it didn't matter how many exams she took, or whether she passed or failed them. A pony cost money to buy and money to keep and, unless they won the lottery, her parents did not have any money to spare. Charlie might not have been much good at maths, but these were sums she could do with her eyes closed.

The school bus stop was at the top of the rutted, muddy lane that led to Folly Farm, and Harry and Larry pushed and shoved each other all the way down it, kicking a pebble between them and fighting to be Harry Kane making his debut for England. At the end of the lane, Larry booted the stone towards Charlie, who ignored it.

'Come on, Thunder Thighs!' shouted Harry to Charlie. 'You should be good at this.'

'Yeah,' taunted Larry. 'With legs like yours, you could be a good footballer.'

'Or a rugby player.'

'Or a tree.'

The boys bent over in hysterical laughter.

'You remember when we put her in goal when she was a toddler?' asked Harry. 'She wasn't too bad until you hit her in the face with a deadly strike. That made her cry.'

'Yeah,' said Larry. 'Then Dad had to put that old riding hat on her head to protect her. Mind you, she saved a few shots with those big legs. I suppose you were better than nothing, Charlie!'

Charlie's cheeks burned as she tried to block her brothers out. She always wanted to join in their games but they told her she couldn't because she was a girl. She held her satchel tightly, hoping nobody would notice what was in it.

'Morning, Harry; morning, Larry!' said Mrs Wheeler as the bus pulled up. 'Morning, Charlie my love. How are you today?'

'I'm fine, thank you, Mrs Wheeler,' replied Charlie, trying to slip by quickly.

'Now, that bag of yours is moving, isn't it?' said

Mrs Wheeler gently. 'Who have we got today – is it newborn chicks or ducklings, or is it Boris again?'

Charlie reluctantly opened her satchel to reveal Boris's sweet black-and-tan face.

'Mrs Wheeler, please let me take him to school. He'll sit under my desk and he won't move and I promise you he'll be really good and we've got maths and he's really good at numbers. *PLEEEASE!*'

Mrs Wheeler smiled. She liked Charlie and she had a soft spot for Border terriers, but she also knew the rules.

'Sorry, love, you know you can't take him to school, especially not smelling like that. Now send him home, there's a good girl.'

Charlie kissed Boris on top of his head, lifted him out of her satchel and set him down on the ground.

'Go on then, go home and I'll see you later.'

With a friendly bark, Boris bounded off down the path back to the farm.

Charlie sighed. 'Right, well, I suppose I'd better get it over with . . .'

*

Charlie was in Year Six, at the primary school beside the 'big school' her brothers attended. As soon as the bus stopped, she ran off to find her best friend Polly. They spent their first lesson of the day – history – drawing pictures of horses and, when the teacher asked them to explain what they were doing, Charlie said, 'Horses were invaluable in every war until tanks came along, Mrs Maxwell. I was just explaining to Polly the different sizes of horse and how they were used for different jobs. This one is jumping over a trench. See?'

She pointed at a drawing of a horse clearing a ditch, hoping Mrs Maxwell wouldn't notice it was clearly being ridden by a girl and that she was not in uniform.

'Ah, yes,' said Mrs Maxwell. 'Very good, Charlie. But if you could concentrate on the subject we're studying today, which is the Black Death, that would be lovely.'

Charlie sighed. History might have been more interesting if they could study the use of horses in medieval England and whether they were immune to the Black Death, but just talking about humans all the time was *so* dull.

When the bell rang, Charlie headed out into the playground. She normally kept to herself at break time. Apart from Polly, the other girls were scary. They all had long hair, which they played with incessantly, wrapping it round their fingers, putting it up and pulling it down, tying it sideways, backwards and on top of their heads. They all talked about music and boys and clothes and things that Charlie didn't really understand. And they teased her. A lot.

'Here she comes, the girl who looks like a cow!' shouted Vanessa Veasey.

The group around her started laughing.

'She smells like one too!' said Serena Tucker. The rest of the girls fell about laughing.

'And look at her hair,' added Vanessa spitefully. 'What do you call that style?'

Charlie ran her hands through her short blonde hair and tried to make it look less like her mother had put a bowl on her head and cut round it – which was exactly what she had done at the weekend.

'Just ignore them,' said Polly, taking Charlie's arm and leading her to the other side of the playground. 'I think your hair is cool. You look like Rita Ora.'

Charlie didn't know who Rita Ora was, so Polly had to show her a picture on her phone. Charlie didn't have a mobile phone, which at her school was almost like not wearing clothes. Everyone else had one and they were always updating to the latest version. They all had Facebook, Twitter and WhatsApp accounts, and they talked to each other using Snapchat, which Charlie always thought was odd as they could just as easily walk across the playground and have a conversation.

'I wish Larry hadn't told everyone about me learning to ride on a cow,' sighed Charlie. 'Nobody ever lets me forget it.'

'You should be proud of yourself,' replied Polly, giving Charlie a hug. 'It must be much harder than learning on a pony. You should come over to my house sometime and try riding Munchkin. I bet you'll be brilliant.'

The thought of riding a real pony cheered Charlie up for the rest of the day, until it was time to go home and take Boris for a long walk in the woods. She told him about the hateful things the girls had said and he wagged his tail sympathetically.

'I knew you'd understand, Boris,' said Charlie, scratching him behind the ears. 'I can't tell anyone else. Mum and Dad would want a meeting at the school and that would only make it worse. And if I told Harry and Larry they'd probably just join in. I know what you're saying.' She looked at his dark eyes, smiling brightly at her. 'Keep going: get through tomorrow and the next day and the day after that. Until I'm old enough to become a jockey – and then I can do what I like!'

Boris ran in a circle round her, barking his approval.

Chapter 2

It was Friday afternoon. Charlie had survived another week at school. It hadn't been easy. Today one of the other girls had put a Post-it note on her back with 'COW' written on it in big letters. Charlie had wondered why everyone kept laughing whenever she walked by, until Polly had spotted the note and whipped it off.

But now her heart felt light at the thought of having the whole weekend at home with Boris and the farm animals. She could read and walk and maybe have a ride on Polly's pony.

'I'm going to a big "Horses in Training" sale with my dad on Saturday morning, but I'll be back after lunch,' Polly told Charlie. 'We could ride then, if you like.'

'I'd love to,' grinned Charlie. 'I'll call you later to arrange it!'

On the bus home, Charlie sat next to the window, straining for a view of the farm gate. As they turned the final corner, she saw Boris waiting at the end of the rutted path. When he spotted the bus, he started to spin round in circles of excitement, chasing his tail. Charlie hopped off the bus and ran towards him, and Boris jumped up into her arms.

Harry and Larry had football practice, so Charlie and Boris walked down the path together, talking about everything that had happened at school that day.

'I just don't get it,' said Charlie. 'Why would there be a number of infinite decimals? And why would you call it pie? I mean, what sort of pie is it meant to be? Chicken and ham? Beef? Or is it a pork pie?'

Boris heard the words 'pork pie' and looked up, but forgot to keep moving. He yelped as Charlie walked into him.

'Oh, Boris!' cried Charlie. 'I'm sorry. I didn't mean to hurt you. You must try not to get under my feet. Silly boy!'

She bent down to rub his side and was rewarded with a very slimy hand.

'Oh, Boris, what have you rolled in now?'

It looked suspiciously like fresh green goose poo. Whatever it was, there was no way he was getting on her bed tonight unless he had a bath first.

'Come on, boy, you know what you need.'

They ran into the house together and, once Charlie had flung down her satchel, scattered her uniform across her bedroom floor and changed into an old boiler suit, she was ready.

Boris glumly followed her out into the farmyard. It seemed he'd worked out what was coming next.

'You are a daft dog,' said Charlie. 'If you didn't roll in so much stinky stuff, we wouldn't need to do this at all.'

Whoosh! Freezing-cold water from the hosepipe hit Boris and he started barking. But instead of backing off or running away from the water, Boris chose to attack it, snapping and growling fiercely.

'He must think it's a snake,' said Mrs Bass, coming out of the house to see what the fuss was.

'A snake spurting cold water!' Charlie laughed.

'How was school?' Mrs Bass shouted over the noise of water and barking as Charlie danced around, trying to apply shampoo.

'Pretty boring,' said Charlie. 'Same old nonsense that won't do me any good, unless I want to open a pie shop.'

'That might not be such a bad idea,' said Mrs Bass as she headed back inside. 'You could help me with the cooking!'

When Charlie finished shampooing Boris and had run him round the big field to dry off, she found her parents in the kitchen with a pot of tea.

On the table were several pieces of paper with red writing on them and a complicated-looking spreadsheet. Her father smiled at her, but she could see the lines of worry on his face as he piled up the papers and put them in a box.

'Hello, poppet, how was school?' he said.

'Fine,' she replied. Boris was at her heels and jumped up into her lap as she sat down. The legs on the chair were a bit wobbly so she had to be careful not to move suddenly, otherwise he would fall off. 'Maths is difficult, but Mrs Maxwell says I'm getting a bit better, and English is OK. We're doing a play by Shakespeare where Richard the Third says he'd give up his kingdom for a horse. I know what he means.'

'Your brains must come from your mother,' said Mr Bass as he patted his daughter on the head. 'Thank the Lord for that.'

He poured her a cup of tea, looked at his wife and then back at his daughter.

'Now, Charlie,' he said. 'Your mother and I wanted to talk to you about something.' He cleared his throat. 'I'm afraid there might have to be some changes at the farm. It's getting harder and harder to make the numbers add up and, what with milk being so cheap, I don't know how much longer we can afford to keep the cows.'

Charlie's mouth dropped open. Her father loved those cows and she knew he would be miserable without Jane Eyre and Madonna and even grumpy old Princess Anne. Mr Bass tried to smile as he carried on talking.

'The boys will be back soon and we thought we might have a family meeting just to let you all know what's happening.'

Charlie nodded, but her mind was racing. It sounded to her as if her parents needed a financial solution – and fast. She liked to think of money-making ideas. This would be fun. Her father was trying so hard to sound positive, but she knew he was counting on her, even if he didn't know it himself.

She resolved to corner her brothers the moment they got home, warn them about the family meeting and see if they had any clever ideas up their sleeves.

She didn't know what nonsense they might come up with, but it was worth a shot.

'And I'll put my thinking cap on,' said Charlie to herself. She really did have a thinking cap. It was an old felt cap that used to be in her dressing-up box. Whenever Charlie put it on, she found she could focus better, as if her brain was linked into an energy force. She finished her tea and headed upstairs to try it out.

After supper (which was meant to be an omelette, but ended up as scrambled egg with bits in it), Mr Bass opened the family meeting.

'As you may know,' he began, looking at his wife, 'it's been difficult recently to make ends meet on the farm.'

Charlie sat up straight in her chair and took a deep breath. 'We need to think creatively,' she said. Her father looked at her in surprise. She went on, before Mr Bass could respond. 'We need to think of something that can earn us money, and fast! Something that makes us stand out from the crowd.'

'I know!' shouted Harry, who always liked to be first with an idea. 'We could have a show, here on the farm. Not like a normal show where all the animals parade round, more like an entertainment show.'

'That's a brilliant idea,' said Larry. 'We could do pony rides.'

'We haven't got a pony,' Charlie pointed out mournfully.

'I know,' said Larry. 'Our pony rides would be really different because they'd be on a cow.'

He beamed with satisfaction. Their parents looked from one child to the next, their mouths open.

'And we could have a dancing competition,' said Harry.

'A dancing competition?' frowned Mrs Bass.

'Yes,' said Harry. 'But for chickens. We can call it "Strictly Come Chicken Dancing" and everyone from around the county can bring their chickens to enter. They could do a waltz or a jive or a foxtrot!'

'A *fox*trot for chickens!' laughed Larry. 'That's genius!'

'I could stream it on my YouTube channel,' added Harry, who was far more interested in computers than animals. 'I bet it'd go viral!'

Charlie shook her head. Her brothers certainly had imagination, if not much common sense.

'What about a bake-off?' volunteered Mrs Bass excitedly. 'I could make lots of cakes and we can sell them in the village shop.'

The children hesitated. None of them wanted to dash her hopes.

'That's a great idea, darling,' said Mr Bass. 'We all love your cakes, but –' he hesitated – 'I don't know that the village is ready for them yet.'

'Exactly!' said Harry and Larry together.

'Besides,' said Harry, 'you'll be too busy running the show to be baking cakes.'

'And,' added Larry, 'we need the eggs for something else.'

He paused and looked around the table, making sure he had everyone's attention.

'There are these painted eggs called Fabergé eggs and they sell for millions of pounds. We just need to paint a few of ours with beautiful colours and we'll make a fortune.'

He sat back and crossed his arms.

'Sweetheart,' said Mrs Bass. 'That's a brilliant idea, but Fabergé eggs aren't real eggs. They're made of gold and precious stones like diamonds and rubies. That's why they're so valuable.'

'Oh.' Larry looked crestfallen.

'You've been very quiet, Charlie,' said her dad. 'Wasn't this whole thing your idea?'

He winked at her to encourage her to share.

'Well,' said Charlie, taking a deep breath, 'it might sound just as crazy, but I think we should buy a racehorse.'

She stopped and looked at her parents. They both seemed surprised, but her mother smiled encouragingly.

'They can win prize money and if they win a really big race, like the Derby, they could be worth millions.' Charlie was excited now and started to talk faster and faster. 'We've got space on the farm and Polly's dad trains racehorses and sometimes you can find a horse who doesn't like being at a big yard like the one Joe's dad worked in and they'd rather have individual attention and I was thinking that we could give them that. As long as they don't mind the cows.'

'Hmm,' said her father when Charlie paused for breath. 'That's an interesting idea, but where could we get one?'

Charlie had done her research.

'There's a "Horses in Training" sale tomorrow in Buffington. Polly's going with her dad. She says it's where they sell racehorses that trainers don't think are getting along as well as they should. I thought we could go, just to have a look.'

Mr Bass put up his hand and said, 'We don't have any money to spend. And even if we did and the horse turned out to be any good, we'd have to sell it to make the profit we need. I'm sorry, love.' He shook his head.

Harry and Larry started sniggering.

'A racehorse?' said Harry. 'Where does she get these daft ideas?'

'I know,' whispered Larry. 'And to think they reckon she's the clever one!'

They both snorted with laughter as Charlie bit her lip and stared down at the notes she'd made. She had worked out a timetable for training, and drawn up a chart including mucking out, grooming and feeding.

'I know how much you want a horse, darling,' said Mrs Bass. 'But we can't afford it. We can barely keep the animals we've got, let alone take on more.'

Charlie pushed back her chair and ran from the room, desperate to hide the tears that were falling down her face. Boris dashed upstairs behind her and she held him tight until she finally stopped crying.

'I know this would work!' she said into his ear. 'If they'd give me the chance, I promise I'd save the farm.'

A little while later, Charlie heard a knock on the door and her mum's voice gently asking, 'Are you all right, darling?'

Charlie didn't feel like talking.

'I'm fine, Mum. Just tired. I'm going to have an early night if that's OK.'

'Sleep well, sweetheart, and see you in the morning,' her mother replied.

Charlie heard a thud on the floor and after her mother had gone she opened the door. There on the ground was a book. It was called *The Greatest Racehorses in the World*. Her mum must have found it in her library and thought it might cheer her up.

Charlie flicked through the pages filled with detailed accounts of horses who had won the best races in America, England, Ireland and France. She read about sprinters, who went as fast as they could for short distances, and stayers, who went steadier, but had the stamina for longer distances. She read about National Hunt horses who jumped hurdles and fences and won races like the Cheltenham Gold Cup and the Grand National, and she read about middle-distance horses who, if they were really good, won the most famous flat race of all – the Derby.

Maybe all was not lost. Maybe she could convince her mother that her idea would work.

That night, Charlie dreamed that she was a jockey in the Derby at Epsom. She was wearing brightly coloured silks and white breeches. She had goggles on her riding hat and she pulled them over her eyes as her mount was led into the starting stalls. She looked down at the jet-black mane of the powerful horse beneath her, and she knew it was a champion. Just as she looked sideways at the other jockeys, there was a sudden loud noise, like the sound of the stalls opening, and –

Charlie woke up with a start. For a moment, she didn't know where she was. Then Boris's black-and-tan face popped up beside the bed. He must've fallen off and woken her up with the bump.

'Oh, Boris, you silly thing! You interrupted a brilliant dream.'

With a soft yap, Boris jumped up again, and Charlie held him tight as she went back to sleep, hoping her dream would pick up where it had left off. She needed to know if she could win the Derby because, if so, this mystery horse could be *exactly* the money-making solution her parents needed . . .

Chapter 3

The next morning was a Saturday and at breakfast the boys were on typical form. Harry grabbed at the toast as soon as it was put on the table, buttering one slice with his right hand while snatching a second piece with his left.

'That's mine too,' he said and then licked it to make sure, before putting it back in the toast rack.

'That's disgusting,' said Charlie.

Harry just grinned at her, while Larry took advantage of her distraction to whip away her cereal bowl and finish what was left.

'You don't need any more food for those thighs!'

Charlie flushed red and ran her hands down the tops of her legs.

'Boys!' said their mum sternly. 'That's enough. Get outside and do the pigs. You never know, you might learn something – Elvis and Doris have got better manners than you two animals.'

Mrs Bass turned to her daughter.

'Your father and I talked about it last night and we couldn't see any harm in him taking you to the sale to have a look at the racehorses,' she said calmly. 'Not to buy anything, mind, but to show him the sort of horse you're thinking about.'

Charlie's face broke into a grin. Maybe her dream had been an omen.

Her day was about to get even better as her mother said, 'Oh, and the boys can stay here. They'll be perfectly happy re-enacting the Stone Age.'

Charlie couldn't understand the point of her brothers, apart from their ability to cause trouble.

'And don't take any notice of their teasing, Charlie. You should be thankful for your legs.'

Charlie wasn't sure she was thankful at all. She wanted to stab her thighs with a fork.

Her mum continued: 'Boudicca, who led her tribe in rebellion against the Romans; Catherine the Great, the Empress of Russia; Queen Victoria; even the two most influential women today – Hillary Clinton and Angela Merkel – do you know what they all have in common?'

Charlie shook her head.

'They all, every single one of them, have powerful legs. And what about Serena Williams and Beyoncé?'

Charlie was interested now.

'Do you think they would have got where they have with thin little legs? And that's before we even start on all your favourite riders! Do you really imagine you could win an Olympic gold medal in dressage or showjumping or eventing without powerful legs? Could you win the Grand National?'

Charlie shook her head, but still said nothing.

'No,' said her mother. 'You couldn't. So be proud of your legs because they will take you far. They will hold you up when skinny legs collapse. Your brothers aren't exactly geniuses, so don't you listen to them.'

Charlie could see them through the window. Harry had grabbed Larry and was trying to judo-throw him into the pigpen. Larry picked up a lump of what looked like pig poo and squashed it into Harry's face. A moment later, they were wrestling in the mud.

'I don't understand boys,' Charlie said, as much to herself as to her mother. 'They just want to fight all the time.'

'Exactly. And that's why they keep on at you – because you won't fight back and they don't understand that. So they tease you and taunt you, hoping for a retaliation. But do you know the best way to deal with it?'

Charlie did not.

'The best way,' said her mum, 'is to do exactly what you've been doing your whole life. Just rise above it. I shall have to put up with them today while you go and have an adventure with your dad. Just make sure you don't spend any money!'

On cue, Mr Bass appeared in the doorway, looking very uncomfortable in a tweed suit that was at least two sizes too small for him.

'All right, little one?' he said with a wink and a hopeful smile. 'Let's have an adventure.'

'Thanks for breakfast, Mum,' said Charlie as she walked out of the kitchen. 'And, you know, thanks for the other stuff too.'

Boris the Border terrier followed hot on Charlie's heels as she and her dad hopped into their battered, ancient jeep. Mr Bass turned the key and the engine coughed. He wiggled his foot up and down on the accelerator and tried again. It spluttered and then stopped. Then there was nothing.

'Rats,' he said. 'I knew I should've got her serviced. We can't take your mother's car because she might need it if those brothers of yours do themselves an injury playing Ninja Warriors.'

'We could take the cattle truck?' suggested Charlie.

'Well, it's not very glamorous, but it's the only way we're going to get there,' said her dad. 'The cattle truck it is.'

They set off for the market town of Buffington, a few miles away. Mr Bass shifted in his seat as he drove. Charlie could see he was uncomfortable in his tweed suit, which was a little warm for the time of year and must be itchy against his skin. Charlie was wearing a pair of jeans that had been handed down from Harry to Larry and then to her. They were worn at the knees and had been taken up at the bottom. They were a little tight on the top of her legs, but they would do. Boris sat next to her, looking attentively at the road ahead.

'Do you think they'll be really expensive?' she asked her father as they bounced along the lane.

'Well,' replied her dad, 'racehorses tend to be the most expensive horses of all, and every one of the bloodstock experts will be trying to find a potential champion. We can play along just for fun, pick one we like and then follow it in the papers for the rest of the year.'

Charlie nodded. The book she'd read about the best racehorses in the world had given her the basics of what to look for. She was also going to use what she'd learned from reading another book her mum had lent her: *How to Find the Olympian Within*. It had taught her that a key ingredient of success was mental approach. She'd known that fitness and talent were part of what made an athlete great, but she hadn't realized that confidence, motivation and knowledge were just as important. You had to be able to handle nerves, to find a way of staying relaxed in tense situations. As far as picking a horse went, Charlie decided that today she would try to work out which one had the mind of a champion.

When Mr Bass and Charlie arrived at the sale, they found it buzzing with activity. Horses were being led into a ring that looked like a mini-theatre. The auctioneer stood on a raised platform with a hammer in his hand and talked so fast that Charlie couldn't understand him.

'*Sixtythousandwe'reatsixtythousandforthislovelyson ofawinner*. I'll take sixty-five, I'll take sixty-five, I say. Thank you, sir. The bid is at sixty-five. Any advance on sixty-five thousand or I'm selling? It's cheap for this lovely horse, but I will sell. Any more?'

He pointed his hammer in the direction of the person who had made the last bid and scanned the crowd for any further interest.

'This is your last chance. Going once, going twice, SOLD!'

He banged his hammer down so hard that Boris gave a squeak of alarm.

'Thank you, Mr Williams. Sixty-five thousand pounds.'

Charlie looked anxiously up at her father, who was starting to sweat. Whether it was the tweed suit or the thought of a horse costing sixty-five thousand pounds, she wasn't sure. With a start, Charlie realized that she recognized the man who had bought the horse. It was Polly's father, Alex

Williams, who was a racehorse trainer. She looked around for Polly, but couldn't see her.

Outside the sales ring there were horses being led up and down, some trotting while two men and a woman watched carefully and made notes in the large sales catalogue they all seemed to be carrying.

'How much for one of those catalogues?' asked Mr Bass.

'Ten quid,' replied a man in a smart red jacket. 'You can buy them over there.'

He pointed to a small wooden hut where a man in a flat cap was handing out the catalogues. Mr Bass fingered the cash in his pocket and looked down at Charlie.

'I reckon we'll save ourselves the trouble, eh?'

Charlie nodded and tried to get a view of the copy the woman in front of her was holding. All she could see was a family tree with some names in bold. The woman had written in spidery lettering: *'Nice type, bit leggy, narrow chest, heart size?'*

'Heart size is really important,' she whispered to her father. 'The average horse heart weighs around three point five kilograms, but a few horses have much bigger ones.'

Mr Bass looked surprised and leaned in closer to listen.

'There was a horse in the eighteenth century called Eclipse. He was unbeaten in eighteen races. When they examined him after he died, the vets found his heart weighed six point three five kilograms. That's double the normal size!'

Her father sucked his breath in and looked more closely at the chest of the horse being walked round in front of him.

'Same thing with Phar Lap,' said Charlie. 'You know, the Australian horse in the film we watched on TV the other week. And the biggest of the lot was Secretariat, who won the American Triple Crown. When he died at the age of nineteen, they found out his heart weighed ten kilograms! That's nearly three times the normal weight.'

'Incredible,' said Mr Bass.

'It is, isn't it?'

'No, you are!' said Charlie's dad as he put his arm across her shoulder and gave her a hug. 'My clever daughter!'

In the far distance, Charlie could see a bit of a commotion. A dark horse was rearing and whinnying, refusing to walk forward.

'I'm going to try and find Polly,' she said to her dad. 'I'll meet you back here.'

Boris trotted along behind as Charlie walked up the hill towards the temporary wooden stables. Even from a distance, she could hear a racket coming from inside one of them.

Charlie looked over the door to see a pony kicking lumps out of the walls. He was clearly angry about something. The dark horse she had seen had his head in the air and was pulling his groom backwards with all his might. She could see the whites of the horse's eyes. He looked terrified.

'Come on, you ignorant beast!' the groom was shouting. 'Move! You're scared of your own bleedin' shadow, you are. It's pathetic.'

Try as they might, the groom and an older man with a grizzled beard couldn't make the dark horse take so much as a step towards the sales ring. As they paused to catch their breath, Charlie asked, 'Who's the pony?'

'It's this one's mate,' said the older man. 'Some of 'em need a sheep or a goat to keep 'em calm. This fella 'as a pony.'

He gave another tug on the leading rein, but the dark horse wouldn't budge. Now that Charlie was up close she could see how beautiful he was. He had a huge chest and a strong neck, his weight seemed evenly distributed over his body and his backside was strong and powerful.

'He's gorgeous,' she said. 'What's he called?'

'Noble Warrior,' said the grizzled-looking man. 'But there's not much noble or warrior-like about 'im! 'E's a coward, so 'e is.'

He walked round behind Noble Warrior and smacked him on the bottom. The horse reared up on the spot, lifting his groom into the air. This was the last straw.

'Eamon, you'll have to deal with him,' the groom said. 'I've had enough of his stupid tricks. I'll take one of the others who might actually want to be sold.'

The groom dropped the lead rein and walked off. Eamon puffed his cheeks out and stepped forward.

Charlie had an idea.

'Do you mind if I get the pony out?' she asked.

'I don't see what good it'll do, but, as 'e's gonna destroy that stable if we leave 'im there, be my guest,' said Eamon. 'They call 'im Percy, by the way. Percy the pesky pony.'

'Hello, Percy, I'm Charlie,' she said as she clipped a rope on to his headcollar and patted his neck. Charlie looked him over. Percy was almost yellow in colour with an even paler blond mane and tail, a white streak down the middle of his face and a pink nose. He had four white socks and one pale brown eye and one that was blue. He was a bit like the palomino pony on her calendar, but with added extras.

'Do you fancy a little walk?' she said calmly.

Percy spotted the gap in the door and barged his way out of the stable towards Noble Warrior, dragging Charlie with him.

'You don't waste time, do you?' Charlie said as she tried to keep up.

Noble Warrior gave a low whicker and dropped his head. The wild-eyed beast of a few minutes ago turned into a calm, gentle horse as he nuzzled the furry pony. As Charlie led Percy forward, Noble Warrior followed him without hesitation.

'Funny-looking thing, ain't 'e?' said Eamon.

'Oh, I don't know,' said Charlie. 'I think he's interesting.'

'Yeah,' Eamon laughed. 'That's what the girls used to say about me. Means the same thing – ugly.'

Charlie gave Percy a pat and led him down the hill. Noble Warrior followed.

As they reached the area just outside the sales ring, people started to laugh.

'Oi, look at this!' shouted a man in a baseball cap. 'We've got a right pair here!'

'How much for the one that shrank in the wash?' asked a woman in a navy blue padded jacket. 'Looks like his colour ran as well!'

She guffawed at her own joke.

The groom who had given up trying to get Noble Warrior into the sales ring suddenly reappeared.

'I thought we'd never get him down here,' he said to Charlie. 'Thanks for your help. You'd better give the pony to me now, otherwise you'll get into trouble with the officials.'

He pointed towards a man with a clipboard who was ticking off names as horses came into the pre-sales ring.

'I understand,' said Charlie. 'But don't let Percy out of his sight. Noble Warrior will be fine as long as he can see him.'

The groom nodded, but Charlie thought he looked embarrassed at having to lead a blue-eyed palomino pony round the sales ring, instead of a racehorse.

Charlie leaned on the white rails to watch Noble Warrior and was surprised that none of the experts, the ones she'd seen taking notes, were taking a closer look. Nor had anyone requested he be checked over. In fact, no one seemed to be bothering with him at all. She beckoned to her father, who was chatting to a vet he knew. Mr Bass walked slowly towards her, moving awkwardly in his tight suit.

'Hello, Charlie. Did you find Polly?'

'Not yet, but, Dad,' she said excitedly, 'you've got to have a look at this horse. He's a bit nervous – he doesn't like being separated from his pony friend – but if we could help him get some confidence, like Victoria Pendleton did before she won her gold medals at the Olympics, then maybe he'd be all right.'

Victoria Pendleton was regarded as too slim and light to be a top cyclist, but she built up the power and then overcame extreme lack of confidence to prove all her doubters wrong. She had started life with skinny legs, but had deliberately developed muscles and stamina to give her strength. For that reason alone, she was Charlie's heroine.

Mr Bass asked the vet if he could borrow his sales catalogue.

'Let's have a look at his page . . . He's a three-year-old colt. That's good. His dad won Group 1 races. That's good too. Says here his mum ran twice and then was banned for refusing to enter the stalls.'

'I bet that's why he's a bit nervous,' interrupted Charlie. 'He gets it from his mum. Good name, though, isn't it?'

'It certainly is,' replied Mr Bass. 'Noble Warrior. That's the name of a champion.' He smiled at his daughter. 'You've got a good eye, my love. Someone might get a good deal here and we can pretend he's ours and follow him all season. I might even take you to the races to watch him run.'

Just then, Eamon tried to lead Noble Warrior into the sales ring without the pony, but, the harder he tried, the more the horse pulled back. He had worked himself up into a muck sweat and was looking a fright. The crowd scattered for fear of getting kicked.

'They'll have to let Percy lead him in,' Charlie whispered to her dad.

She saw Eamon approach the man who had the list. He then went to the auctioneer, who looked less than impressed, but eventually Charlie heard him say, 'Well, fine, if it's the only way.'

Amid much disdain from the crowd, Eamon led Percy the pony into the ring, followed by Noble Warrior – a thoroughbred who was supposed to be a racehorse. Although he had calmed down, Noble Warrior looked dejected. He had lost his lustre and his swagger.

'What'll we say for this regally bred son of a Group 1 winner?' asked the auctioneer. 'He's a fine-looking animal, no doubt about it. No runs to his name yet, but it's only a matter of time. Wonderful pedigree, has impressed some of the leading trainers in the country. Who'll open the bidding for me?'

There was a low murmur in the auction ring as people chatted to one another, but no one made a bid.

'Come on, come on!' said the auctioneer, raising his voice. 'Surely someone can see the potential here. Let's start the bidding off at five thousand pounds. Five thousand, four thousand, three thousand, two thousand . . .'

For every other horse that had entered the ring, the auctioneer had gone up in price, but this time he was dropping it at lightning speed. Yet still no one wanted to bid for Noble Warrior. Charlie couldn't understand it.

'One last chance,' the auctioneer said. 'I'll take a thousand pounds.'

At that moment, Charlie finally spotted Polly on the other side of the auction ring, standing beside her father, Alex Williams. Charlie raised her hand to wave at them.

'Thank you!' shouted the auctioneer. 'A thousand pounds I'm bid and I will sell. Any further bids?'

In horror, Charlie realized that the auctioneer's hammer was pointing right at her. She looked up at her father, whose eyes had widened to the size of saucers. He swallowed hard as he grabbed her hand to stop her waving again. But it was too late.

'Going once, going twice, SOLD to the young lady in the blue jeans.' The auctioneer bashed his hammer down and then pointed it again in Charlie's direction.

'Gosh,' said Charlie quietly.

'Gosh indeed,' said her dad, swallowing again. He let out a huge sigh. 'Well, we'd better hope you're right about him.'

'I'm so sorry, Dad. I didn't mean to.'

A stern-looking woman collared Mr Bass before he and Charlie had a chance to move. He wiped his forehead as he read the paper she handed him and fumbled in his pocket for the credit cards that he'd brought in case of an emergency.

'I'll have to s-split the p-payment,' he stuttered.

'A split payment is perfectly acceptable,' said the woman. 'Just fill out your details, your card numbers and sign here. That's it. Good luck, sir, and thank you for your business.'

Leaving her dad to shake hands, Charlie thought she'd better make the best of things. She and Boris ran up the hill to find Noble Warrior, who was following Percy back to the yard.

'You'll need a large enough stable for the both of 'em,' Eamon said in a gruff voice.

'What do you mean?' replied Charlie.

The man grinned. 'Think of it as one of them deals at the supermarket – buy one, get one free!'

Charlie was stunned. It took her a couple of seconds, but then she understood: Percy the pony was included in Noble Warrior's price. She hugged a surprised Eamon and squealed with delight.

'Wait till my dad realizes we've got a bargain! A racehorse and a pony, all for a thousand pounds! He'll be so pleased. And, for what it's worth, I don't think Percy is ugly and neither are you.'

Eamon blushed and handed her a small folder.

'There's 'is passport – Noble Warrior's, I mean. 'Is vaccinations are up to date and 'e's all set.'

Charlie was busy examining the paperwork as she heard Eamon say, 'Good luck!'

But she also thought she heard him mutter, 'You'll need it . . .'

Chapter 4

Noble Warrior and Percy the pony were now the property of Bill and Charlie Bass. Charlie led Percy back to the cattle truck and Mr Bass followed with Noble Warrior, who seemed exhausted after the rigours of the sales ring.

Polly and her father helped them lower the ramp and watched as Percy hopped on board, followed a little hesitantly by Noble Warrior.

'I can't believe you've got a pony too,' exclaimed Polly. 'Now we can go riding together and do gymkhanas and hunter trials and be a team.'

Charlie's heart swelled with excitement at the thought.

'Let me know if you need any help, Bill,' said Alex Williams. 'You've got a nice type there, if you can sort him out.'

Mr Bass was very quiet on the journey home, but Charlie made up for it, chattering away about the fields they could use for Noble Warrior's slower work and where they might take him for his faster gallops.

'I can supervise his exercise in the morning before I go to school, and I think we should take him out in the evenings as well for a gentle canter and a walk in the woods. That might suit Noddy. Is it OK if we call him Noddy at home? I think it sounds friendlier than Noble Warrior. Anyway, we could make a gap in the fence between the Long Acre field and the side of the hill. That way we'd make a gallop long enough for him. And then I think we should take him down to the stream because the book I read said they took Red Rum to the seaside and bathed his legs in the cold water and that helped him win three Grand Nationals.'

As they turned off the main road on to the potholed drive that led to Folly Farm, Charlie opened her door to let Boris out and he ran ahead, barking to tell the family they were home. By the time they had negotiated the bumps of the drive as slowly as possible, a full welcoming party was waiting for them in the farmyard.

Mrs Bass, Harry, Larry and Joe were all there. Her dad climbed down gently from the driver's seat while Charlie threw herself out of the passenger side.

'How was it?' asked Mrs Bass. 'Did you have fun?'

'Fun might be one way of putting it,' said Mr Bass as he swallowed hard.

'Mum, Mum, wait till you see what we've bought! We've got a champion in here!' shouted Charlie.

She ran round to the back of the cattle truck to take down the ramp. Her mother followed, saying, 'I thought you were just looking. You weren't meant to buy anything.'

'It was a bargain,' Charlie replied, at exactly the same moment her father said, 'It was an accident.'

Harry and Larry stood there, elbowing each other, while their mum helped Charlie undo the bolts and lower the heavy ramp.

Mrs Bass stared at the pale, fat pony.

'That's our champion?' she asked disbelievingly.

'No!' said Charlie. 'Percy came free. Wait until you see Noddy, who's behind him.'

'NODDY?' cried Harry and Larry in unison.

'You can't have a racehorse called Noddy!' said Larry.

'OMG, what's that?' shrieked Harry, pointing at Percy. 'Ugly bugly or what?'

'Idiots,' said Charlie.

Climbing up into the truck, she gave Noble Warrior a pat and whispered in his ear. 'Just ignore them. I do. Now, come and meet Joe; he's going to be your friend.'

Charlie untied Percy's rope from the ring on the side of the truck and led him down the ramp. Noble Warrior followed meekly behind.

'Two of them?' said Mrs Bass. 'You weren't meant to be buying anything at all and you've come back with a horse *and* a pony. What on earth have you been up to, Bill Bass?'

'It's a long story,' said Mr Bass. 'But the good news is that we got two for the price of one.'

He smiled hopefully.

'That may be,' said his wife. 'But I don't think they'll share their food or their rugs or their vet's bills, will they? And where are we going to keep both of them?'

Joe had been listening.

'The barn would work,' he said. 'It's a great big space so they can share it. There's lots of straw and I think it'll be just fine . . .'

Joe trailed off as he caught sight of Noble Warrior for the first time. His face lit up.

'Isn't he a beauty?' he said softly. 'Lovely head and look at those shoulders and backside! He's got power all right. Look at the chest on him too! Plenty of heart room there.'

Joe stroked the side of Noble Warrior's face and scratched behind his ears. Noddy lowered his head and submitted himself to a gentle massage.

Charlie stood with Percy as everyone looked admiringly at Noble Warrior. Everyone except Harry, who seemed more interested in the pony. He started making faces at Percy, poking out his tongue and waving at his blue eye to see if it was blind.

'Harry, leave him alone, will you?' said Charlie protectively.

She needn't have worried. As Harry tried to squeeze the skin on his neck, Percy shifted his weight, lifted his front leg and brought it down hard on Harry's left foot.

Harry stifled a scream and tried to move from under the pony's hoof, but he was trapped. Percy moved his hoof from side to side, grinding it on Harry's foot.

'Help!' yelled Harry. 'He's going to break my toes!'

'Sorry?' said Charlie, cocking her ear towards Harry. 'I didn't catch that.'

'Get him off me . . . PLEASE!'

Charlie took two steps forward and said in a calm voice, 'Walk on, Percy. Good boy.'

The pony walked obediently forward as if nothing had happened at all, leaving Harry hopping on one leg, his other foot clutched in both hands.

MOOOO!

The loud voice of a particularly moody cow sounded from the milking shed.

'It's Madonna,' said Mr Bass. 'Five o'clock on the dot and she wants milking. You'd think that cow had an actual clock on the wall. She'll set them all off now.'

Sure enough, the other cows joined Madonna in a chorus of moos.

'Right, let's get moving. Joe – you take Noddy and Percy to the barn. Charlie, you get them some hay and a bowl of nuts. Harry and Larry, you start the milking while I take this wretched suit off, and you and I, my love,' he said, looking at Mrs Bass, 'had better have a chat . . .'

Later that afternoon, Charlie joined Joe in the old barn. The sun was dipping in the sky, throwing a warm light on the two four-legged friends and their new home.

Joe was grooming Noble Warrior and with every stroke of the body brush, followed by a shine with the stable rubber, the gleam on the thorough-bred's coat started to show.

Charlie swung herself up on to the gate that Joe had put across the front of the open barn, her legs dangling as she shared carrots from the garden. Percy was a greedy little blighter, snatching them from her hand, but Noble Warrior was much more polite, taking a carrot gently and tickling her hand with his muzzle as he did so.

When Joe had finished, he gently threw the blanket Charlie had brought from her room across Noble Warrior's back.

'There you go, son, that'll keep you warm for the night. Now, don't you mind all the noises those cows will make. I'll be back bright and early in the morning for milking and I'll make sure you get your feed. Then, who knows . . . ?'

He drew Noble Warrior's head into his chest and pulled his ears gently.

'You'll have fun riding Percy, Charlie,' continued Joe. 'He'll be much easier than riding a cow, I can tell you that. I'm happy to give you lessons.'

'Would you?' said Charlie. 'That would be amazing.'

'Teatime!'

Mrs Bass's voice echoed across the farmyard and Harry and Larry charged out of the milking shed, almost knocking each other over in the rush to get to the kitchen. Joe and Charlie took their time, reluctant to leave their new charges.

As she walked into the kitchen, Charlie heard the tail end of her parents' discussion as they stood by the Aga.

'I still don't know what possessed you. And who's going to ride him?' Mrs Bass was asking. 'He's too big for the boys and you can't do it.'

'I'm sure it'll all work itself out,' Mr Bass said. 'And, if it doesn't, someone will just have to work it out for me.'

Charlie felt a pang of guilt. It was her fault. She hadn't realized she was bidding when she waved at Polly and she certainly hadn't realized how much her wave would cost. Part of her wished she could get a refund, but another part was convinced that Noble Warrior could not only earn more than her father had spent, but that he could win enough to get the farm back on track.

And, as far as riding him was concerned, she knew *exactly* how to solve that problem . . .

Chapter 5

Charlie woke suddenly in the middle of the night. Boris was sitting up, his head cocked towards the window. Outside she could hear strange noises from the pigs, and the chickens were clucking as if a fox might be on the prowl. She pulled on her jeans and trainers, grabbed a jumper and quietly slipped downstairs with Boris creeping behind her.

'Shh now, no barking,' she said as she silently opened the front door.

Clang!

Charlie froze at the sound of a bucket being knocked over. What was going on? Had horse rustlers come to steal Noble Warrior? Maybe someone had seen him at the sale yesterday and followed them home. Or perhaps it was thieves hoping to lift a few bits of farm machinery they could sell on? She had read in the local newspaper about a spate of farm thefts.

Creeping forward, Charlie found the bucket and saw vegetable peelings on the ground. Someone had definitely kicked it over. Pausing for a moment to let her eyes adjust to the darkness, Charlie noticed that the door to the shed where the cows' food was stored was hanging open. And she could hear noises inside – strange crunching noises ...

The wind picked up, whistling through the trees and making the buildings creak. Charlie shivered. She inched forward and peeked through the doorway. Through the gloom, she could just make out a pale, ghost-like shape.

Boris darted forward and growled.

'Boris, no!' hissed Charlie. 'Come back here.'

The pale shape turned and looked straight at Charlie. Then it made a noise. A low, soft whicker. Immediately, she felt the tension drain from her body.

'Oh, Percy, it's you! Naughty pony. How have you got out?'

Charlie walked towards the pale little pony and put her arms round his neck. Percy was perpetually hungry and, having finished off his share of hay and the rest of Noble Warrior's as well, he must have decided to find more food.

With Boris yapping at Percy's heels like a sheepdog, Charlie led him back to the barn, where she found the gate hanging open. Percy had chewed through the string that had kept it in place.

Noble Warrior was standing quietly at the back of the barn, looking confused. Percy was clearly pleased with himself.

'You mustn't break out,' said Charlie as she closed the gate. 'You might get lost in the dark.'

She looked around to see how she could keep the gate shut and decided the best option was to ram a bale of hay against it so that Percy couldn't push it open. *How to Find the Olympian Within* included a chapter on weightlifting and Charlie knew that female weightlifters not much taller than her had raised more than double their own body weight above their heads. From what she had read, it seemed that leg power was as important as arm power. She looked down.

'Come on then, thunder thighs. It's time to put you to the test.'

Charlie squatted down beside the bale of hay and pushed. It slid reluctantly. She pushed again. And again. Slowly, it inched towards the gate and, ten minutes later, it was in position. She sat on the bale and puffed out her cheeks. Then she crept back to the house and went back to bed.

As morning dawned, Boris stretched and licked Charlie's face. Despite her late-night adventure, she was wide awake in seconds.

'Come on, Boris,' she said. 'We've got chores to do.'

Charlie pulled on Larry's old jeans and a rugby shirt, and ran downstairs in her socks. She didn't own any jodhpurs or riding boots, so jeans and wellington boots would have to do.

She paused at the kitchen door. Her mother was speaking in a low, urgent voice.

'If this doesn't work out, Bill, we'll be in real trouble. I've just got the latest bills and it's worse than I thought. If we can't start paying them off soon, we risk losing the farm and our whole way of life. I can work from a town if I have to, but you and the kids – you'd be miserable anywhere else.'

'I know, love,' replied Mr Bass. 'But I'm sure it won't come to that. I know we made a mistake, but what's done is done. And it might work out for the best. Charlie thinks we've got a champion on our hands and I believe her. Only time will tell.'

Charlie sucked in her breath. She hoped she was right about Noble Warrior.

Pulling on her boots, she made her way to the barn. Percy had his head through the gate and was munching on the bale of hay she had heaved into place last night.

'You are the greediest pony in the world,' she said. 'Honestly, if I don't keep an eye on you, you'll be as big as one of our cows.'

Percy turned his head sideways and slid it back through the gate. He looked at Charlie with his shiny blue eye, which twinkled with mischief. He was naughty and clever, which is a dangerous combination in a person or a pony.

'So, how are we all?' said Mr Bass with a cheery smile as he walked over. 'What's this hay bale doing here?'

Charlie didn't feel the need to tell her dad everything that had happened in the night so she just stuck to the bare essentials.

'Oh, the string won't keep the gate shut so I put this across for now.'

'You dragged this here on your own?'

Charlie nodded.

'That's my girl,' said Mr Bass. 'I always knew you'd be a strong one. Said it to your mother the day you were born. This one will be a winner, I said.'

He smiled to himself as he looked over Noble Warrior. 'You sure did cost a lot,' he said, 'but boy oh boy, you're a beauty. Mind you, handsome is as handsome does, so we'd better find out what you're made of. The only question now is, who's going to ride you, eh? I'm too heavy. Harry and Larry are too young and too reckless, and Mum has never ridden in her life.'

'I've been thinking about that, Dad,' said Charlie. 'What about Joe?'

'Joe's a farm boy, not a jockey,' said Mr Bass, shaking his head. 'Anyway, I don't think he'll want to, after what happened to his dad.'

'Well, actually, sir, I would like to. If you'll let me.'

Joe was standing behind them in his farm overalls and boots, a bag in his hand. He didn't look much like a jockey, but there was a fierce determination in his eyes.

'Please let me try. I've got all my gear and everything.'

He started unbuttoning his overalls, which were peppered with a week's worth of milk, cowpats and grass stains. Underneath he was wearing a close-fitting top and light brown breeches. From the bag came a pair of shiny brown leather boots and a black crash hat, covered in a red silk cap. He had an old leather saddle with girths and a saddlecloth, as well as a bridle that looked as if it had seen better days.

'It's my dad's old tack. It's not much, but I think it'll do and, if I clean it every day, it'll get soft again. I polished these last night,' he whispered, showing them the boots. 'I always wanted to be a jockey, you see, but then it all went a bit wrong after my dad died. Mum couldn't bear to see the horses on the gallops every morning, so we came down here and then I had to get a job, so I ended up milking cows. Not that I mind milking cows, sir,' he said rapidly. 'It's just . . . You know, back then I felt I could do anything. Be anything.'

'Well, lad,' said Mr Bass kindly, 'I don't see why not. Your dad was a good jockey so maybe talent runs in your family. Let's give it a go and see what happens.'

Joe's face lit up as if he'd been given every Christmas present he had ever wanted. He walked over to Noble Warrior and patted him gently on the neck.

'You and me, boy. It's you and me,' he said as he tacked him up, adjusting the bridle to fit his head and gently doing up the girth round his tummy.

Mr Bass gave Joe a leg-up and he landed softly in the saddle so as not to frighten Noble Warrior or put too much pressure on his back. Then Charlie led Percy out of the barn and Noble Warrior followed meekly behind. They walked through the farm, past the pigs and the chickens and the cows. Jane Eyre mooed as she watched the procession and Princess Anne glanced at them disdainfully, but the others ignored them.

Harry came out of the farmhouse with a piece of toast in one hand to see what was going on.

'Who's that with the fat pony? Thunder Thigh Thelma?'

'Shut up, Harry,' said Charlie.

'Hey, boys, want to come and see a racehorse gallop?' said Mr Bass.

Harry shoved the entire piece of toast into his mouth, leaving a line of jam on his top lip.

'Yeth, pleathe.'

'Let's hop in the jeep. I worked out what was wrong with it the other day. No diesel.' Bill shook his head. 'Expensive mistake that turned out to be. Anyway it's working now and we'll need it to keep up. A racehorse can gallop at over thirty-five miles per hour, you know. Amazing animals.'

Noble Warrior was perfectly happy following Percy. When Charlie started to run and Percy broke into a trot, Noble Warrior trotted behind them, but if Joe tried to take him anywhere on his own he planted himself to the spot. However much Joe talked to him, kicked him gently but firmly, tapped him down the shoulder with his stick, Noble Warrior would not budge.

Joe turned him in a circle and tried again.

'Come on, boy, let's just have a little canter up the hill. We've got to see how fast you are and we've got to get you fit. Come on!'

He kicked and coaxed, urged and begged, but it was no good. Noble Warrior wouldn't move.

Charlie stood holding Percy with a leading rein. She couldn't run fast enough or far enough to lead him for anything more than a short trot.

Mr Bass was starting to look worried. No wonder no one else wanted to bid for what appeared to be such a well-bred horse.

'Looks like you've bought a dud, Dad,' said Larry. 'We'd have been better off with Strictly Come Chicken Dancing and those painted eggs.'

Harry turned on his little sister.

'Great idea, Charlie! Let's buy a racehorse that costs a fortune, but, better than that, let's buy a racehorse who doesn't gallop!'

Charlie's eyes started to fill with tears. She didn't want to be the one who let her parents down. She didn't want to be the reason that they ran out of money and had to sell the farm.

'Did you say he'd go wherever Percy goes?' asked Mrs Bass, who had heard the hubbub and had come out to watch.

'Yes,' replied Charlie in a wobbly voice.

'Well, in that case, we need to find a way to make that work.'

'I know!' Harry shouted. 'Let's put the ugly pony in the jeep and drive in front of Noble Warrior. Then he'll try to keep up.'

'Don't be stupid,' said Larry. 'We can't put a pony in the jeep. Where's he going to sit?'

Although the suggestion was a daft one, it gave Mr Bass an idea.

'How do you fancy riding Percy bareback?' he said to Charlie. 'It'll be easier than riding Ermintrude and I know you're strong enough to stay on. Let's put those legs to the test.'

He threaded a plait of baler twine through one side of Percy's headcollar, passed it over to the other and tied it in place, creating a makeshift pair of reins. Then he lifted his daughter on to Percy's back and put on her head the same riding hat he'd used when she was a toddler goalkeeper. Except now it fitted perfectly.

'That'll have to do for now,' Mr Bass said. 'Just sit tight and grip with your legs, OK?'

Charlie nodded.

'Be careful,' said her mother.

Charlie nodded again, although she wasn't sure that 'being careful' was really possible in this situation. She looked at Joe.

'Any advice?'

'Take a handful of his mane,' he said. 'That'll help you keep your balance. Don't try to do much, stay relaxed and concentrate on keeping yourself right in the middle of his back. Lean back a little bit and just go with the rhythm. It'll be fine.'

Charlie nodded at Joe. He made her feel calm and more confident. She had to be able to do this. She had to.

Her dad patted her on the leg and turned to Joe.

'You keep Noble Warrior down here until Charlie's got halfway up the field. Turn him to face the other way so he doesn't see Percy's gone. Then let him go.'

Taking a deep breath, Charlie urged Percy into motion.

Mr Bass drove the jeep alongside as they cantered up the field. Charlie clung on to Percy's mane for extra balance and squeezed as firmly as she could with her legs.

Harry leaned out of the car and shouted, 'Come on, Thunder Thighs, grip tight!'

Percy put his ears back flat and bared his teeth at him. Charlie slid to one side of his tummy and forced herself back into the middle.

'Shut up, Harry!' she muttered.

'You're doing great!' shouted their dad from the driving seat. 'I'll stop here, but you keep going for as long as you can.'

He looked back to the bottom of the field where Noble Warrior was not standing still or looking calm. He'd realized that Percy had gone without him and now he was spinning in a circle, rearing and bucking, desperate to catch up. Joe was doing an amazing job of staying on his back as he held the reins tight to stop him from tearing after his little friend.

Mr Bass cupped his hands round his mouth and yelled as loud as he could: 'OK, JOE – LET HIM GO!'

Joe relaxed the reins and Noble Warrior took off at such a pace that he was nearly thrown backwards out of the saddle. The horse thundered up the field, eating up the ground. Joe sat as low as he could, making his body streamlined, his chin just above Noble Warrior's mane.

Clinging on to Percy for dear life, Charlie looked over her shoulder as, with every massive stride, Noble Warrior got closer. He flew past the jeep, leaving Mr and Mrs Bass, Harry and Larry all gasping, and, thirty seconds later, he was level with Percy.

As soon as he was, Noble Warrior put the brakes on. He went from thirty-five miles per hour to nought in two strides and Joe was thrown forward over his neck. The young jockey clung on and pushed himself back into the saddle.

Charlie was amazed. Percy had just cantered as far as his round belly would take him and was puffing with the effort. Noble Warrior was hardly blowing at all.

'How was that?' she asked.

'*Un-be-leev-able!*' said Joe, his face one big grin.
'This horse is an aeroplane!'

The rest of the Basses came chugging up in
the jeep.

'Well, well,' said Mr Bass, smiling at his family.
'Looks like we've got a racehorse on our hands.
Now all we have to do is make him want to gallop
on his own.'

Then Charlie understood why no one else at the
sales had been interested in Noble Warrior and

why Eamon had been so keen to get rid of him. He might have been bred to be a racehorse, but he didn't want to run: he just wanted to be with Percy.

But, thought Charlie to herself, *if we can work out a way to make one desire help the other then all our problems are over!*

Chapter 6

Charlie went to school the next day on a cloud of adrenalin. She couldn't wait to tell Polly about her weekend.

'You cantered bareback up the field?' asked Polly in amazement. 'Wow, that's really impressive. Your legs must be killing you.'

'Not really,' said Charlie. 'They're fine. You should have seen Noddy, though. He's faster than lightning.

And I can't wait for you to meet Percy. He's the most beautiful pony you've ever seen.'

Charlie struggled to concentrate in school until it came to geography. They were studying spa towns. Mrs Maxwell was off sick, so Mr Morrison the deputy head was standing in for her. He was tall and thin, with glasses perched precariously on the end of his nose.

'Bath, Boston Spa, Royal Leamington Spa, Malvern and Epsom have all attracted many visitors over the centuries,' he droned. 'Can anyone tell me something about those towns?'

Charlie's hand shot up. She had done some research since they got back from the sales with Noble Warrior.

'Charlotte, gosh, your hand is up. That is a rare occurrence. Please, go ahead,' said Mr Morrison.

Charlie took a big breath and then said, as fast as she could, 'Epsom is famous for the Derby. It's a mile-and-a-half race for three-year-old colts and fillies, but fillies don't run in it very often because they have the Oaks the day before. It's one of five

Classics in the country and it's the most famous of the lot and there are derbies all over the world, in France, Germany, Ireland and even America, but THE Derby is the one that's run at Epsom in June. It was first run in 1780 and this year it's going to be won by a horse called Noble Warrior.'

Charlie paused and glanced round the room. Her classmates looked stunned and Polly was grinning widely.

'That's excellent, Charlotte,' said Mr Morrison, scribbling something down on a piece of paper. He liked watching the racing and was partial to a little bet every now and then. 'What did you say the name of that horse was?'

'Noble Warrior,' said Charlie. 'He's at our farm and I'm training him for the Derby.'

'Oh,' said Mr Morrison, and his face fell. He stopped writing. 'Well, that's nice. So, who can tell me a bit about Bath?'

The day couldn't go fast enough for Charlie. All she wanted was to get back home to see Percy and

Noble Warrior. She had planned their evening exercise and was eager to see if she could get Percy further up the field before Joe and Noddy set off in pursuit. She also wanted Joe to try to keep Noble Warrior in a steadier canter as he would have to learn not to go all out from the start if he was to last the full mile and a half of the Derby.

When they were doing maths, Charlie worked out how many times they would need to canter round a field of just over a hectare to cover a mile; in science, she analysed how much protein she should add to Noddy's feed to give him the correct nutritional balance for an athlete; and in art she drew a picture of a horse galloping, his mane and tail floating in the wind.

By the time Charlie was on the bus home, her head was bursting with ideas of how to improve Noble Warrior's training to get him ready for the Derby. She didn't have time for her usual chat with Mrs Wheeler about what her family was up to, and even Boris, who was sitting as usual at the end of the drive, was surprised at the speed with which she ran through the ruts to the farm.

She left Harry and Larry pushing each other towards the electric fencing in a game they liked to call 'Shock'. It never ended well.

'Mum!' shouted Charlie as she clattered through the front door. 'Mum!'

'I'm right here, darling,' said Mrs Bass gently. 'I can hear you perfectly clearly. Now, why don't you sit down and tell me what you want.'

'We need to work out a training regime and a diet,' said Charlie breathlessly.

'Why? Are you planning to run at the Olympics?'

'Not for me! For Noble Warrior! He can run in the Derby, you see, because he was entered as a foal. I saw it on the paperwork that came with his passport. Some horses, if they've got good breeding, get entered as soon as they're born and that's what happened with him. It won't cost much more to actually run in it this year, but we need to get him properly fit. You've read all those books about great athletes – can you help?'

'Leave it with me,' said Mrs Bass. 'I'll see what I can find in my library.'

Charlie knew that her mum's library wasn't *actually* a library or even somewhere with bookshelves. It was a room with about fifty different piles of books. It looked completely chaotic, but Mrs Bass knew exactly which book was in which pile and where. The trick was to slide the book out without the whole pile collapsing. It was like a giant game of Jenga.

'Visitors!' shouted Harry and Larry in unison as they arrived in the kitchen. They'd obviously survived the walk home, although Larry's hair was standing wildly on end.

Outside in the farmyard was a bright red, spotlessly clean Range Rover Evoque. Charlie had never seen a car without a single speck of mud. Polly's mother slid effortlessly from the front seat and placed her suede boots carefully on the cobblestones, avoiding the muck and puddles.

Polly hopped out from the other side and opened the boot.

'Hello, Mrs Williams,' said Charlie politely.

Polly's mum looked immaculate, her hair freshly styled and a cashmere wrap thrown casually over her shoulders. Charlie glanced at her own mother, who was looking a little uncomfortable in her faded cords and battered trainers. The family always joked about Mrs Bass's clothes being pre-loved, but now Charlie saw how much her mother would prefer a brand-new outfit, one that had never been worn by anyone else but her.

'Lovely to see you, Jasmine. Can we help with anything?' said Mrs Bass.

'Well, actually,' said Mrs Williams, 'I think *we* might be able to help *you* . . .'

She smiled kindly as she explained that Polly had told her about Charlie riding Percy bareback.

'I know it's probably good for your technique, but –' she paused as Polly came from the back of the car, carrying a saddle over one arm and a bridle in the other – 'we wondered if maybe you wanted to use these?'

Charlie's mouth dropped open.

'Wow! A proper saddle and bridle! Oh, thank you, thank you so much.'

'Um, y-y-yes,' stuttered Mrs Bass. 'They look lovely. Um, how much, um, how much do we owe you?'

'Nothing at all,' Mrs Williams said. 'Polly used them a few times on Munchkin. They don't fit any more, but I don't really want to sell them on. I'd much rather someone we know was using them. So Charlie can borrow them for as long as she needs to. It would be our pleasure.'

'Gosh, well, I mean, thank you,' said Mrs Bass. 'Would you like to come in for a cup of tea? I've made some cake.'

'Who could refuse an offer like that?' smiled Mrs Williams.

'Oh, plenty do!' said Charlie. 'But you might enjoy it. You never know!'

She laughed as she led Polly off to the barn. Noble Warrior stood with his head over the gate, his ears pricked as he watched the pigs snuffling about in the mud. Percy couldn't see over the gate, but he could put his head through the gaps.

'He'll be wondering what they're eating,' said Charlie. 'All he ever thinks about is food. Isn't he gorgeous?'

'Well,' said Polly, 'he's certainly unusual. One of a kind, I'd say.'

Polly showed Charlie how to fit the bridle.

'If he won't take the bit,' she said, 'just slide your finger between his lips at the back here and he should open his mouth.'

Next she showed her how to tighten up the cheekpieces so that the bit sat comfortably in Percy's mouth and then turned her attention to the saddle.

'There's a numnah that goes underneath the saddle so it won't rub his back. You keep it in place by putting the girth straps through this loop ... And then you can put the buckles of the girth on the straps, like this.

'You go round to Percy's left side,' she said to Charlie. 'It's called the nearside and you have to always get on and get off from there. Now, take the girth –' she passed it under Percy's tummy – 'and let's see if it fits.'

After a bit of loosening on Polly's side and pulling on Charlie's, they eventually made the girth meet the buckles. Percy was a little grumpy about the whole episode, but he also looked different.

'I think he's even more handsome now he's got his tack on,' said Charlie, standing back to admire her pony. 'It makes his tummy look a little less obvious.'

'I know what you mean,' said Polly. 'Once you're riding him regularly, I bet the weight will drop off him. He probably didn't get much exercise before, if he was just a companion pony.'

Charlie tied Percy up to a metal ring her father had nailed into the wall.

'I'll be back soon to take you for a ride,' she promised.

Percy looked at the carrot he was offered as a low-calorie treat and wolfed it down in two bites.

Polly and Charlie wandered back into the kitchen to find their mothers deep in conversation.

'Well, the thing is, Jasmine,' Mrs Bass was saying, 'I had no idea the costs would just keep mounting. I – Oh, hello, girls.'

Charlie frowned. She knew she had made a mistake in bidding for Noble Warrior, but she hadn't even thought about all the other expenses. She hoped it wasn't *too* much.

'As I was saying,' Mrs Williams picked up without hesitation, 'general naughtiness you'll have to put up with: that's just how it is with ponies. As for Noble Warrior, he'll be a bit delicate because he's a thoroughbred, but I expect he'll like getting lots of individual attention. He won't have had that before.'

Charlie thought that sounded very positive. Maybe she could still make this a success, despite the cost. After all, if Noble Warrior won the Derby, their problems would be solved. She decided to try and focus on the good points.

'The tack fits Percy,' said Charlie. 'We had to try a few times with the girth because he always blows his tummy out, but I can just get it on to the first hole and then, if I walk him round a bit, I can tighten it up to hole three and that's safe, Polly says.'

'Excellent news,' said Mrs Williams, rising from her chair and brushing off the dog hair from the back of her trousers.

'Right, Miss Polly,' she said. 'You have your own pony at home that needs riding so we'd better get going. Thank you so much for tea, Caroline – I've never had carrot and green bean cake before. It was . . . what's the word?'

'Inedible?' suggested Charlie.

The mothers both laughed.

'Unusual,' said Mrs Williams. 'But I'm not sure I'll be trying it at home!'

As Polly and her mum walked back to their gleaming Range Rover, there was one more surprise.

'Oh, yeah,' said Polly, handing Charlie a bag and getting in the car. 'I brought these too. Just in case you need them. No bother if you don't; just give them back to me at school. Thanks for letting me meet Percy and Noble Warrior. They're both gorgeous! See you tomorrow.'

Polly pressed a button to lower her window and waved all the way down the drive as her mother slowly negotiated the puddles and ruts. When they were out of sight, Charlie looked into the bag. Inside was a crisp pair of jodhpurs, a pair of brown jodhpur boots without a single crease in the leather and the very latest riding hat.

'This must be a mistake,' said Charlie to her mum. 'I thought she was giving me stuff she didn't need any more, but these all look brand new. I don't understand . . .'

Mrs Bass put her hands on Charlie's shoulders, looking her directly in the eye. 'Some people have lots of money but no heart; some people have lots of heart and no money; and a few people have both. Mrs Williams and Polly are two of the latter and we're very lucky to know them. Now, go and put your jodhpurs on. You've got a racehorse to train.'

Chapter 7

Joe was waiting in the barn with Noble Warrior tacked up and ready. He was brushing quarter marks into the horse's bottom, sweeping a body brush down across the hair, then sideways across half of it and then diagonally to create shark's teeth. Noble Warrior's coat gleamed as if it had been polished.

'You look smart!' Joe exclaimed as Charlie opened the gate.

'New kit,' she said. 'My friend Polly gave it to me because she thinks I ought to try to do things properly. We've got tack now as well!'

She pointed to Percy, who looked very cross about having a girth round his tummy and was playing with the bit in his mouth, putting his tongue over and under it as if he was licking a lollipop.

'So I see,' smiled Joe. 'If those posh yards in Newmarket could see us now, they'd be quaking in their boots. We've got the top team down here at Folly Farm.'

Using a bale as a mounting block, Joe leaped into the saddle and gave Noble Warrior a pat.

'Nice easy evening exercise, my boy. Nothing to get excited about. Just you, me, your friend Percy and my friend Charlie. Off we go.'

As they walked across the farm, Mr Bass came out of the milking shed.

'Off for another ride, are you? Don't overdo it now.'

'It's all right, Dad,' said Charlie. 'Mum found a book on getting fit. It was about a marathon runner, but she's adapted it for Noble Warrior and we've got it all mapped out. It's six weeks to the Derby so we need to ramp it up gently. We'll do a bit of trotting and a steady canter in the evenings, plus twenty minutes standing in the brook. That'll keep his legs nice and tight.'

'OK,' said Mr Bass, taking off his stained baseball cap that said 'Cows Forudder' and scratching his head. He didn't understand a word his daughter was saying.

'The Derby?' he shouted after them. 'What do you mean?'

But Charlie was already out of earshot.

Next morning, after the cows had been milked and Noble Warrior had done his morning exercise, Joe was sitting in the kitchen, eating his breakfast and reading the *Racing Post* while Harry and Larry squabbled over the last piece of toast.

Joe was looking at an article about that year's Derby. One Irish trainer had a horse who had already won the English 2,000 Guineas, another who was favourite for the Derby Trial at Leopardstown in

Ireland, and was thinking of running two more who had no chance of winning, but would set the gallop for the others. They were known as pacemakers.

'It's ridiculous!' exclaimed Joe. 'Seamus O'Reilly has got ten horses in the Derby. Ten!'

'Actually, I need to talk to you about this, Dad,' said Charlie.

Mr Bass glanced up from the adverts for second-hand tractors in *Farmer's Weekly*.

'What, love?'

'We need to pay the next entry stage for the Derby. It won't cost much because Noddy's already on the list. Look, here he is.'

She pointed to a page full of horses' names. 'It's lucky that he's already entered. His original owner, the one who actually bred him, must've done it because he thought he was going to be a winner.'

Mr Bass looked at his wife and swallowed hard.

'How much exactly will it cost?'

'Only a couple of hundred pounds, I think,' replied Charlie. 'And I can help. I've got some coins in my piggy bank upstairs.'

'I don't want you spending your savings, Charlie,' said Mr Bass. 'You've earned them. We can find another way, I'm sure we can.'

He looked at his wife.

'I could still try selling cakes,' she said.

'NO!' shouted everyone at once.

Charlie knew this was an all-or-nothing gamble, but she also knew that in Noble Warrior they had a very special horse. If they could just make him want to gallop on his own, she was convinced he could be a champion.

'I know we've got to pull together. I've heard you talking,' she said, looking at her parents. 'I realize we're in trouble, but I also think Noddy can help. He can win the Derby – I know he can.'

Harry and Larry looked at each other. They had no idea what their little sister was going on about, but it sounded serious.

'You're not expecting us to chip in, I hope?' Larry asked, clearly worried. 'I've been saving up for a cricket bat.'

'And I need a new HD webcam,' said Harry, instinctively clasping at his pockets.

'Don't worry,' Charlie replied. 'I don't want your money, but I would quite like your help. Harry, I need you to go online and see if you can find a race for Noddy. It has to be in the next two weeks. And not too far away because the cattle truck doesn't like long journeys. It needs to be for three-year-olds and probably over a mile and a quarter, just short of the Derby distance. Paula Radcliffe never ran a full twenty-six miles right before the London Marathon so we'll do the same. Save him for the complete distance until the day itself.'

Harry frowned. Charlie could sense that he wasn't sure why she was asking him. But she had read in *How to Find the Olympian Within* that to get team members on your side you had to give them a sense of responsibility and ownership. She needed Harry and Larry to be partners with her, to make them care as much as she did, and to do that she needed to trust them with something important.

'OK,' said Harry, still a little suspiciously. 'I'll see what I can do.'

'And, Larry,' Charlie continued, 'I wondered if you would start investigating the opposition? It's crucial we find out how good the other horses are and who Joe should follow in the race. Why don't you start by looking through all those old copies of the *Racing Post* by the back door? There are statistics on all the jockeys and you can work out who the best ones are.'

'OK, Lady Muck.' Larry doffed an imaginary cap and backed out of the room, mocking her as he went.

Charlie wasn't sure whether she would ever get her brothers to feel a real part of the team, but she knew she had to try. She was well aware that Harry thought it was a daft idea to have a racehorse in the first place and he certainly didn't have any time for Percy. But she was hoping the boys might get interested because of the facts and statistics. They liked football and they knew all the stats for the Southampton players. Maybe they could feel the same about racing if they just understood it a bit more.

Leaving them to get on with their work, Charlie headed out to the barn to give Noble Warrior his breakfast.

On his wife's advice, Mr Bass had done a deal with a local arable farmer to swap milk and eggs for oats. So Noble Warrior had oats for breakfast every day, with a dash of linseed oil, a handful of fresh carrots from the garden, some honey, soaked barley and, occasionally, a raw egg.

The eggs were Charlie's idea. She'd read about Nijinsky, the Derby winner of 1970, who was put on a special diet which included a raw egg every day and half a pint of stout. It helped him to win the St Leger, the final Classic of the season, and so complete the Triple Crown of Guineas, Derby and St Leger. No colt had done it since, so the diet must have worked. They didn't have any beer on the farm so it would just have to be eggs. Not every day, mind, just now and again. Noble Warrior also got a handful of fresh clover with his hay, which Charlie picked especially. And her mum had recommended that once a week he should have a bran mash to give him the carbohydrates needed to fuel his muscles.

'And you need plenty of fuel, don't you, boy?' whispered Charlie, stroking the racehorse's soft flank. 'So you can go like a rocket . . .'

It was the middle of the afternoon when Harry ran out into the farmyard and yelled, 'Guys, we need a meeting!'

Mrs Bass was feeding garden titbits to Elvis and Doris the pigs, Mr Bass was checking Madonna for mastitis and Joe was practising his 'jockey style' on two crates outside the milking shed, with Charlie beside him holding a stopwatch.

Joe had one foot on each crate, his knees bent and his body crouched forward like a downhill skier. He tried to hold his position for three minutes, pushing with his arms and moving his body for the last minute and a half. He was clicking his tongue and whistling through his teeth.

'What on earth are you doing?' asked Harry.

'He's practising,' Charlie said. 'The Derby will take a little over two and a half minutes to ride so I'm making sure he can last for three minutes, just to be sure. Thirty seconds left!' she shouted.

Joe increased the tempo of his pushing, crouching lower as he did so.

'Well, that's lovely,' said Harry, 'but we've got things to discuss, so he'd better finish his race quickly and both of you can canter on into the kitchen.'

'I've got good news and bad,' Harry said. 'Charlie asked me to find a race for Noble Warrior between now and the middle of May. By the way, did you know that there are hundreds of types of horse race, over loads of different distances? To enter some, the horse has to have won a race; for others, they have to have *never* won a race; for another, they have to have cost a certain amount at the sales. And then there are these things called "handicaps", where the best horses have to carry extra weight, which I think sounds really unfair.'

Larry yawned loudly.

'Get on with it, would you?'

Harry scowled at him and continued.

'There's a race at Salisbury that looks just right for Noble Warrior, but we have a few problems.'

Charlie and her mother exchanged looks. They had never seen Harry so serious or so concentrated. Trusting him with an important job really seemed to have worked.

'First, Charlie, you need to take out a permit,' Harry said. 'That's like a licence to train, but not as expensive. Next, we need to make sure Noble Warrior is up to date on his vaccinations. Third, we need to pay the next entry stage for the Derby so that he can actually run. Finally, we need to register a set of colours.'

Mrs Bass interrupted.

'Darling, that's all lovely, but everything you've mentioned costs money and we don't have very much.'

Harry was unfazed. 'I've added it all up so you can see what costs what.'

The whole family looked at Harry in stunned silence as he swivelled his laptop towards them. On the screen was a chart showing not just the amount of money needed for Charlie's permit, the final entry stages for the Derby, the vaccinations and the colours, but also the amount it would cost in diesel to make the journey to Epsom and the costs of the race at Salisbury.

Given that Harry had got an F in his GCSE mock exam in maths, he was suddenly showing a remarkable grasp of arithmetic.

The total was £4,000.

'Gosh,' said Mrs Bass. 'That's a bit steep, isn't it? Is that everything? Could it end up being more?'

'No,' said Harry. 'It shouldn't. I've included a crisis fund for emergencies – vet's bills and things like that.'

Mrs Bass started doing calculations in her head. She looked at Mr Bass and winced.

'I've still got my savings,' said Charlie. 'I really don't mind. In fact, I'd like to contribute.'

'I'll put mine in as well,' said Harry.

Charlie could hardly believe her ears.

Larry blew out his cheeks and sighed.

'Oh, all right, then,' he mumbled. 'I'm in too.'

'With all three of you helping, we could just about do it,' said Mrs Bass, looking grateful. 'But only just.'

'What made you change your mind, Harry?' asked Charlie.

'This,' he replied, pulling up a new chart on the computer.

It was a list of numbers. There were a lot of noughts. The family all leaned in around the kitchen table and it took a few seconds for them to register what they were looking at.

'It's the prize money for the Derby,' explained Harry. 'This is what we could win.'

'*A million pounds?*' five voices said together.

'That's a million for the winner, with ten per cent going to the trainer, which is you, Charlie, and about the same going to the jockey,' explained Harry. 'The rest goes to the owner. If you finish second or third, it's less, but there's also the value of the horse to consider. If Noble Warrior wins the Derby, he'll be worth millions more as a stallion.'

'A million pounds,' Mr Bass repeated under his breath. 'A million pounds . . .'

'We could buy season tickets to watch Southampton in the Premier League!' shouted Larry.

'We could build some proper stables!' cried Charlie. 'And I could buy Polly a really nice present to say thank you for giving me all her riding gear.'

'I could get a new tractor,' said Mr Bass. 'And a hundred more cows!'

'I'd buy a new set of tack and a better bike to ride to work,' added Joe.

'I'd pay off *all* the bills,' said Mrs Bass. 'Then I'd get myself a sports car.'

'A sports car?'

Charlie was perplexed. She'd never seen her mother take any interest in cars at all.

'Yes. A Jaguar XK Coupé with a five-litre V8 engine, six-speed automatic transmission, dynamic stability control, performance braking system and touch-screen display.'

A shocked silence fell over the kitchen as everyone digested this outpouring of information.

'Which book are you copy-editing at the moment, Mum?' asked Charlie.

'*Life in the Fast Lane: A History of the Sports Car*,' answered her mother. 'Why?'

The whole family burst out laughing.

'Oh, Mum,' Charlie said. 'You are funny. Do you know what would be great, though? We could build a proper library for all your books. I'd help you put them in different sections and we'd make sure they were in alphabetical order as well.'

'Maybe that's a better idea,' Mrs Bass nodded. 'I'm not sure a sports car would cope with our drive.'

'First things first,' said Harry, still using his grown-up organizer's voice. 'If Noble Warrior is going to run at Salisbury, we have to decide who owns him and what the colours will be.'

'Well,' said Mr Bass, 'Charlie's the one who found him and bid for him, so she should probably be the owner. But then your mother and I paid for him, so maybe *we* should be the owners, with Charlie as the trainer. Oh, I don't know . . .'

Charlie considered the options. Although it was tempting to claim outright ownership of Noble Warrior, she wanted everyone to feel involved. That way she knew they would all work harder for the best outcome and everyone would enjoy it more.

'I'm happy to be the sole owner of Percy,' she said, 'as I don't think anyone else wants him.'

'You're right there!' interrupted Harry.

Charlie continued: 'But Noddy belongs to all of us. I think we should register him as being owned by "The Bass Family". And Joe, that includes you.'

Joe puffed out his chest with pride.

'We do have one more problem,' said Harry slowly. 'Joe doesn't have a jockey's licence.'

'What?' gasped Charlie.

'Oh, no!' exclaimed Joe. 'I hadn't even thought about that. How do I get one?'

'I know about this,' interjected Larry. 'I read about it in the *Racing Post* when I was looking up all that stuff you told me to find about jockeys. There's a course at the British Racing School that you have to go on, and then you have to pass a test.'

'But that'll take too long, won't it?' said Joe.

'Too long for you to be ready for Salisbury, yes,' Larry said, thinking as fast as he could. 'But not too long for Epsom. If you go straight to Newmarket next week, hopefully your licence will come through in time for the Derby.'

'What will we do if I don't pass? Or if it doesn't come through in time?' Joe asked quietly.

Charlie put her hand on his arm and said calmly, 'That won't happen, so don't even think about it.'

She sounded full of confidence, but inside her stomach was churning. She started to bite the inside of her lip as she thought about the consequences. If Joe couldn't ride, they'd never get Noble Warrior to the start, let alone the finish, and then it would all be over. The race, the farm – everything.

'Let's get you registered on that course as soon as we can,' said Mrs Bass. 'And don't worry. Charlie will make sure Noddy is ready for you as soon as you come back.'

Mr Bass pushed back his chair and stood up. Then he leaned forward in a crouch position and started pushing with his hands.

'Bill, what on earth are you doing?' said Mrs Bass.

'Well, someone will have to ride Noble Warrior while Joe is away, and I think it's very clear who that person should be!'

Then, with a particularly vigorous push, he overbalanced and fell flat on the kitchen floor.

Chapter 8

'Dad, sit tight!'

Noble Warrior was spinning himself in a circle with Mr Bass trying desperately to stay in the saddle. Harry and Larry were either side of the frantic racehorse, holding on to one rein each to help control him. Their father clutched at the horse's mane and clamped his legs as tight as he could, but, from her vantage point halfway up the hill on Percy, Charlie could see his balance was going.

Suddenly she saw Larry let go of one side and Harry get flung in the air as Noble Warrior reared. Her father, who hadn't ridden for twenty years, was thrown backwards and landed in the wet grass.

'Ow!' he said, rubbing his backside and stretching his left leg. 'That hurt.'

Noble Warrior took off, riderless, as fast as he could go. A minute later, he was happily back beside his palomino pal. Charlie reached out to catch his reins. He didn't pull away or shy, but was perfectly happy to be led. As long as he was with his friend, he didn't mind whether he was ridden, led or loose.

'It's OK, Noddy, it'll all be fine. Dad didn't mean you any harm.' Charlie soothed Noble Warrior as best she could, gently whispering to him. 'We would never leave you behind. I promise.'

Having settled him down, Charlie headed back down the hill to check on her father. He was standing up, but he looked pale and in pain.

'I don't think I've broken anything, but I'm not sure I should try that again. He's just too much for me.'

'Makes you realize what a good horseman Joe must be,' said Larry.

'And I bet Noddy misses him,' Harry agreed.

Charlie was formulating a new plan. Noddy would need a fast gallop or two just before his race at Salisbury, but in the meantime she could concentrate on building up his stamina for the week that Joe was away.

She'd seen photographs of polo ponies being exercised in a biography of the Duke of Edinburgh her mother had shown her. One rider would lead four or five ponies at a time and exercise them all together. That's what she'd do with Percy and Noble Warrior.

Charlie may have been only ten years old, but her physical strength and her confidence had multiplied in the weeks she had been riding. Now that she'd got used to being in the saddle every day, she could happily ride with only one hand on the reins. Percy had changed too. He was now sleeker and, as the nights had got warmer, so his furry-looking hair had fallen out, leaving a gleaming golden coat underneath.

'I'll need a long rope,' she said to Larry. 'Can you plait some baler twine together so it's good and strong? Harry, you can take Noddy's saddle off because we won't need that any more. I'm going to treat him like a polo pony.'

Larry quickly fetched the newly plaited rope and threaded it through the rings of Noble Warrior's bit. He handed the end to Charlie, who took it in her left hand.

'I'll take him for a trot as usual and then we'll canter for as long as Percy can last,' she said. 'It won't be fast for Noddy, but it'll keep him moving and a week of long, slow exercise might not be a bad thing.'

'As long as I don't have to get on him again, I'm happy!' said Mr Bass, still rubbing his bottom.

'I think he feels the same way, Dad,' grinned Larry.

Mr Bass took the boys in the jeep into the middle of the field to keep an eye on his daughter and their precious charge. Noble Warrior had changed personality completely. The horse who had been flinging himself all over the place a few minutes ago was now jogging along happily beside Percy.

Charlie broke into a gentle canter, trying to copy the Olympic gold medallist Charlotte Dujardin who she'd seen sit deep in the saddle with a straight back and long legs. It was a more secure way to ride than sitting up like a jockey and it was much better for leading another horse.

Noble Warrior took a second or two to work out what he was supposed to do before he started to canter as well. He stayed absolutely level with Percy, not trying to compete with him, just loping along, his one big stride equal to the pony's two. Boris ran along behind them, stopping occasionally to sniff at something and cock his leg, then rushing off to bark at a pheasant, before bombing back to join the gang.

Charlie smiled as the morning light gleamed on the grass – and that's when the idea came to her. Noble Warrior's colours should be green and gold! Green was a good, positive colour and gold had a sense of glory about it. She imagined Joe in a green jacket with gold edging and a gold cap. That would look really smart and it would go well with Noble Warrior's jet-black coat.

It was going to be perfect!

For the next six days, Charlie and Percy exercised Noble Warrior before she left for school and took him out again in the evenings. Larry helped her with mucking out their bedding in the barn, and with grooming both horses so that their coats were kept clean and healthy. Charlie missed Joe, but she was enjoying spending time with her brother. They had never really chatted before because Larry had always been poking fun at her. Now she realized he was quite good company. Some of his jokes were even almost funny now the punchlines weren't all about her 'thunder thighs'.

She checked Noble Warrior's legs every evening, feeling for any signs of heat, which might indicate a tendon strain or a bone splint, but they always felt cool and smooth to the touch, with no sign of swelling.

One evening, while Charlie was checking Noble Warrior, Harry walked cautiously into the stable. Percy bared his teeth and huffed out his breath loudly.

'Hey, Harry, what's up?'

'I, um, well, I . . . wanted to have a chat.'

'Sure thing,' said Charlie. 'About what?'

'Well, it's not you I want to talk to actually. It's Percy.'

Harry looked embarrassed as he tilted his head towards the palomino pony. Percy's blue eye fixed him with a steely glare. Harry cautiously put his hand out. The pony took a step away.

'I know we got off on the wrong foot,' said Harry. 'But could we, you know, maybe start again? I'm sorry I said you were ugly.'

He stroked Percy's golden neck and the pony relaxed.

'Now you've got rid of all that yellow fur, you're actually quite a smart-looking pony,' Harry continued.

Percy swung his head round and biffed him in the stomach.

'Ouch!' said Harry, laughing. 'Point taken. Anyway, I've come to give you an update on

Salisbury. There are seven other horses entered and we've got to declare as definite runners by ten o'clock on Thursday. The green-and-gold colours have been approved and I've provisionally booked Bryan Dennis to ride.'

'Bryan Dennis?' said Charlie in surprise. 'The champion jockey?'

'Yes,' replied Harry proudly. 'The horse he was supposed to ride has torn a muscle and his agent was impressed when I told him Noble Warrior is entered in the Derby.'

'Wow! Good work, Harry,' said Charlie.

'Oh, and I spoke to Joe too,' added Harry. 'He's doing really well and is getting a lift back from Newmarket on Tuesday night – in Alex Williams's horsebox!'

'That's brilliant news,' said Charlie. 'When will we know if he's got his jockey's licence or not?'

'Good question,' replied Harry. 'Hopefully, in time for the Derby, but it might be touch-and-go.'

Carefully lifting the gate back into place, they headed to the kitchen together.

'Dad,' said Charlie as they came inside, 'when Joe gets back, can we take Noddy to Mr Williams's gallops? He needs to do a fast gallop over at least a mile before the race at Salisbury, and it would be good for him to go somewhere new.'

Mr Bass nodded and touched the peak of his baseball cap.

'Righto, guv'nor. I'll get on to it straight away.'

Chapter 9

Noble Warrior was the first to welcome Joe back to Folly Farm. He whickered gently as he heard Joe's footsteps on the cobbles of the farmyard. The horse had an ear for footstep patterns – the uneven stride of Mr Bass, the eager trot of young Charlie, the heavy steps of Harry or Larry and the gentle, even pace of Mrs Bass. Joe was lighter on his feet than any of them and that's how Noble Warrior knew his friend was home.

'Hello, old boy, how have you been?' asked Joe, pulling the horse's head into his chest and wrapping his arms round his neck. 'Oh, I've missed you, I have. I rode some great horses up there in Newmarket – winners – but they're not a patch on you.'

Percy muscled in for a group hug, his twitching lips nuzzling into Joe's pockets for hidden titbits. But their dawn greeting was interrupted by insistent mooing from next door. The sun was rising and the cows had made their own way to the milking shed.

'Right, you two, I'll be back in an hour or so. Those cows wait for no man.'

Joe pulled on his overalls and boots and started attaching the milking machines. For once, the cows seemed quite content. Even Madonna and Princess Anne were in a good mood. As he was finishing off with Scarlett O'Hara, Joe felt a cold, wet nose on his arm. It was Boris, wagging his tail and smiling up at him.

'Hello, boy,' laughed Joe.

Boris scampered back out of the milking shed, yapping and dancing in a circle.

'He's in there, is he? Good boy, you found him.'

It was Charlie, dressed in her new jodhpurs with a neat jacket and crash hat.

'Hey, Joe, how was the British Racing School?'

'Well, I learned a lot and there were some really good instructors,' he said, lifting his head back from under Scarlett O'Hara's tummy. 'But I'm happy to be home. Do you know what? Noddy recognized my steps, I swear he did! He was whinnying even before he saw me. And even Percy was pleased to see me, although I suspect that's because I had Polos in my pocket!'

As Joe finished off milking, he told her all about his course.

'There's this electronic horse you sit on while you watch a race,' he said. 'It's got a racing saddle on it and everything, so you can practise riding a finish. It was really good, but I missed you all.'

He patted the last cow on the rump and sent her back out into the field.

'I missed Noble Warrior most of all. They haven't got a horse to touch him, honest they haven't.'

'And what was it like?' Charlie asked carefully. 'You know, being back where your dad died?'

'It was weird for the first couple of days, when I went past the house where we lived, but then one day I was out running and suddenly I was there, right where he had his fall. I hadn't meant to go anywhere near that gallop, but I wasn't concentrating and it just happened. So I stopped and thought about him and I felt that I could talk to him, so I told him what we were up to with Noble Warrior and that I wanted to ride him in the Derby. Then I felt really calm, like he'd given me his seal of approval or something. When I started running again, I felt happy – you know, properly happy, maybe for the first time since he died.'

'I think it was probably a good thing that you went there,' said Charlie thoughtfully.

'Yeah,' Joe replied. 'Me too. Then that evening I went to the pub where Dad used to go with his mates and there they all were. We started talking about him and they told me funny stories of the things he got up to. We were all laughing and it felt really nice, just to be able to talk about him without being sad. They're all really excited, by the way. They had a look at Noble Warrior's price for the Derby and he's a thousand to one, so they've all put a little bet on him, just as a way of remembering Dad and supporting me, I guess.'

'Wow,' said Charlie. 'Looks like it won't be only our lives he changes if he wins.'

'Oh,' said Joe, reaching into his bag. 'And they gave me this.'

He held out a blue-and-red striped stick. It had a rubber handle and a soft leather flap at the end of it.

'It's my dad's whip. I know Noddy won't ever need me to use it, but I thought I'd carry it anyway, just for luck.'

As they walked back to the barn, Charlie filled Joe in about all the exercise she'd been doing with Noble Warrior and explained that they were going to Alex Williams's yard that morning.

'We need to do some fast work: a racing-paced gallop over a mile or so,' she explained. 'And we need to see if he'll gallop with other horses because we can't put Percy in the race at Salisbury!'

They laughed at the idea of Percy lining up at the start. He'd probably try to kick the other horses. Then they arrived at the barn and Joe had a long look at Noble Warrior.

'He looks really well, Charlie. You can see that he's strengthened up and filled out a bit, and look at his coat! He's gleaming!'

'That's down to Larry,' said Charlie generously. 'He's been helping me with the grooming and he's really got the hang of it. He's even been practising his plaiting for race day.'

'Larry's been helping?' Joe sounded surprised. 'Next you'll be telling me that Elvis and Doris have learned to fly. Talking of pigs, has Noddy been eating well?'

'His bucket is always clean as a whistle, but I don't know if that's because Percy gets in there to lick it out! He's had oats and a raw egg every other day, plus a bit of linseed oil, and I'm thinking of giving him a banana after exercise – that can help recovery because it replaces blood sugar.'

They chatted away comfortably as they got Noddy and Percy ready for their journey to the gallops. Joe protected Noble Warrior's legs with bandages and covered his tail to keep it clean. Just as they finished, the rumble of an engine told them that Mr Bass had the cattle truck ready and waiting.

'I'll stay back here with them,' said Charlie, leading the horses up the ramp. 'You go up front with Dad, Joe, and tell him all about Newmarket.'

After half an hour, they turned through a large set of gates with 'Cherrydown Stables' written across them in bronze. It was just before seven o'clock. If everything happened on schedule, they would be away by eight thirty, in time to drop Charlie off at school on the way home.

Inside, there seemed to be hundreds of people in matching black jackets with 'Cherrydown' written in gold on their backs. They were sweeping yards that already looked clean, carrying buckets of water and some had saddles under their arms.

Mr Bass parked the cattle truck next to three slick-looking black-and-gold horseboxes and lowered the ramp on to a raised platform that had been built specially to allow the horses a gentler descent. Percy was so keen to explore this smart new yard he practically dragged Charlie down the ramp.

'Wow!' she said when she saw the first of four large quadrangles of stables. Normally, there was a strict 'no children' policy in the yard so, whenever she had been to stay at Polly's house, which was about a mile away, they had never come here.

The stables were spacious and had high ceilings, with windows at the back and the front. Charlie could see little fans whirring in the corner, to keep the air fresh.

Joe jumped into the truck to untie Noble Warrior and led him gently into the yard, next to Charlie and Percy.

'What are those?' Charlie asked, pointing to what looked like mini-doors on the outside wall of the stables.

'That's so the person in charge of feeding can check whether the horses have eaten up without

135

going into the stable,' Joe explained. 'You know how Percy charges at you every time you come in with the feed bucket?'

Charlie nodded.

'Well, imagine half a ton of racehorse doing that. This way, they don't have to walk into the box with a bucket of feed. The flap just opens up and the manger is attached to it. It's quite clever.'

Mr Bass finished closing up the cattle truck and followed them in.

'Hey, Bill, good to see you!' Mr Williams was wearing a red jumper and black trousers. He had a pair of binoculars around his neck and a clipboard in his hand. 'I've just got to get Second Lot out and I'll be right with you.'

He took a whistle from his pocket and gave three loud toots. On cue, horses started appearing from different yards and making their way to the central area, where they stood.

'Jack, you'll go one steady and then work up the Valley Gallop with Neil. Make sure they finish nicely together. Stacey, take Tania and Brian with you and make sure that filly doesn't get left behind. Tom, can you lead Taffy and Storm? Peter, you set a good strong pace and let Chrissie come up and join you at the two-pole. Don't let them slacken off.'

Mr Williams carried on until he had spoken to all fifty riders. Charlie looked at their faces and saw the concentration. Although Mr Williams was a bit like a teacher in front of a class, they were far more attentive than she ever was in school. She could see by the grizzled look on some faces that they had been racing for a long time, but some of the younger riders seemed not much older than Harry and Larry. She counted quickly and worked out that thirty of the riders were men and twenty were women.

'Right, that leaves you, Nigel. I'd like you to look after Joe and Charlie over here. I've given her special permission to be in the yard today and I know she'll be on her best behaviour. And Joe here is going to be a star, so I hear.'

'Thanks again for the lift home from Newmarket, sir,' said Joe politely.

'Happy to be of service,' replied Mr Williams. 'Now, Nigel, they'll tell you what they need to do with the horse, but make sure you show them all the best bits of Cherrydown. I don't want them going home with a bad impression!'

'Nice-looking horse, that,' Nigel said to Joe as Mr Williams walked off to supervise the other riders. 'How did you get him so fit?'

Joe motioned towards Charlie.

'You'd better ask the trainer.'

Charlie explained their recent routine and the weeks of work they had done before that to build up his muscle and core strength.

'Sounds like you need to do a bit of fast work,' said Nigel. 'Start steady and then really let him stretch out so he opens up his lungs and you can find out what sort of an engine he's got.'

'That sounds perfect,' agreed Charlie. 'The thing is, he's a bit insecure without Percy so I need to position myself carefully.'

Nigel stared at Charlie, who was mounted on the palomino pony and looking very serious.

'How old are you?' he asked.

'I'm ten, nearly eleven.'

'Same age as I was when I first came here,' said Nigel. 'That was in Mr Williams Senior's time. He was a strict man, he was. If he saw a spot of mud on your boots or a piece of straw in a horse's tail when you were riding out, he'd send you back to the yard.'

He looked around him and gestured to the green slopes, the trees and the other horses.

'But how could you not want to do your best in a place like this? I didn't mind the discipline and I wanted to be here all the time, so I left school when I was fourteen and I've been here ever since.'

'That's amazing,' said Joe. 'You must have ridden hundreds of different horses.'

'Oh, I've seen all sorts, that's for sure,' said Nigel as he patted the neck of the horse he was riding. 'Good and bad ones, fast and slow ones, keen ones and lazy ones. They come in all shapes and sizes and you just don't know how good they'll be until you get them on to the gallops.'

Charlie held her breath. They were about to find out the truth about Noble Warrior. Had she been right? Was he special? Could he be a champion?

Nigel, Charlie and Joe fell in line at the back of the queue of horses walking out of the yard and into a wide avenue with beech trees on either side. The riders chatted to each other as their horses loosened up. A few of them swished their tails to swat away flies and flicked their heads back, but generally they seemed very relaxed and calm.

'Jockeys, sit tight!'

The shout came from the front and was relayed back down the line to Charlie and Joe, and soon the whole line was trotting. A few of the riders with short stirrups sat up and forward, keeping their weight out of the saddle.

Percy gave a little squeal of excitement. After all his training with Noble Warrior, Charlie suspected that he'd started to think he was actually a racehorse. They trotted up the hill on a woodchip path, which was soft under the horses' feet. As they climbed higher, they started to see the view across Hampshire, Wiltshire and into Dorset. To the south, Charlie caught a glimpse of the sea and to the north nothing but green fields, trees, hills and villages. There wasn't a major road in sight and the sound of horses snorting was all she could hear.

Until Percy chose that moment to contribute his own musical accompaniment, breaking wind with every trot stride as if playing a trumpet. Charlie blushed and tried to pretend it wasn't happening.

'Good little tune there,' said Nigel as he smiled kindly at Charlie.

When they got to the top of the hill, they found Mr Williams and Mr Bass waiting, having driven up in a 4 x 4. Mr Williams consulted his clipboard again and looked closely at every horse, checking none of them were lame and making sure the right pairs were together.

Nigel described to Joe and Charlie exactly where they would go.

'We've got a mile gallop that will be just right for what you want. We can go steady for the first four

furlongs, then let him breeze home for the last four. It starts over there,' he said, pointing, 'goes in a big left-handed sweep and finishes up the hill over there.'

Charlie looked at the field carefully. There were little black plastic bushes stuck in the ground to mark out different gallops. The gallop Nigel had suggested was almost a P shape. If she could cut the corner from the start of the gallop to the end of the tail of the P, her plan might work.

Mr Williams and Mr Bass hopped back in the 4 x 4 to position themselves near the end of the gallop, from where they could see the horses finish. Charlie went to the start, to make sure Noble Warrior set off with his lead horse.

Joe shorted up his stirrup leathers as he'd been taught at the British Racing School and patted Noble Warrior on the neck. The thoroughbred was starting to sweat.

'Nothing to worry about, old boy,' Joe whispered. 'Just a little piece of work and we'll be going home again.'

Nigel was one side of Noble Warrior, Percy the other and, as they got to the eight-furlong marker, Joe nodded to Charlie.

'Go now,' he said. 'See you at the finish.'

He clicked his tongue against the roof of his mouth and urged Noble Warrior to keep moving forward. Noddy obliged, staying close to Nigel on his horse.

'That's a good lad. Off we go.'

As the two of them broke into a gentle canter, Charlie grinned. She'd been right. Noble Warrior had become so used to cantering alongside Percy on the lead rein, he'd just assumed that Percy was right behind them.

Instead, Charlie wheeled him round, gave him a kick in the belly and was soon thundering back towards her father and Mr Williams. Despite having little legs and a fat middle, Percy was pretty fast and was nearly at the end of the gallop just as Noble Warrior turned the corner at the far end.

Alex Williams had his binoculars trained on Joe and a stopwatch in his hand. He clicked it as Noble Warrior passed the four-furlong marker.

'He's got a lovely stride on him. Nice and balanced. That boy of yours looks very neat,' he said to Mr Bass, looking at his watch. 'Just under twelve seconds for the furlong. That's pretty standard.'

Charlie frowned. 'Pretty standard' wouldn't win the Derby. Noble Warrior obviously needed some more encouragement. Digging in her heels, she moved Percy into the middle of the gallop so that Noble Warrior would see him.

The effect was electric.

'Blimey!' exclaimed Mr Williams. 'That's some turn of foot.'

He looked at his stopwatch again and whistled through his teeth as Noble Warrior galloped faster and faster. Nigel was left far behind as he thundered up the final two furlongs. Charlie turned Percy up the hill and cantered off, hoping Noble Warrior would follow.

Joe passed the last furlong marker in a blur as Mr Williams clicked his stopwatch and looked at the time.

'That can't be right,' he said. 'I don't believe it.'

'What?' asked Mr Bass. 'What's wrong?'

'He just did the last four furlongs in under forty-four seconds. I've never seen that in my life. You've got a machine here, Bill. A machine. Did you say he's entered in the Derby?'

'Yes, he is,' said Mr Bass. 'We've got to pay the final entry stage tomorrow. Do you think we should?'

'Absolutely!'

Noble Warrior was blowing hard at the end of the gallop, but he recovered quickly and his heart rate was back to normal just ten minutes later.

Charlie and Joe chatted the whole way back to the yard about how Bryan Dennis should try to ride him at Salisbury. If he could make him relax in the early stages, that final burst of speed could be delayed until the crucial moment.

Then Charlie looked at her watch and gasped. It was quarter to nine! She was going to be late for school!

They loaded the horses back in the cattle truck and set off as quickly as they could. By the time they reached Charlie's school, it was well past nine and everyone should have been in lessons. But instead all the pupils from both the primary school and the secondary school were in the car park, lined up in years.

Charlie groaned.

'Must be a fire drill,' said Mr Bass. 'What luck! You won't have missed anything.'

'Yeah,' muttered Charlie. 'And no one is going to miss us in this.'

Sure enough, as the cattle truck drove into the school, the boys in Year Ten started whistling.

'Nice wheels!' shouted one. 'What's your other car? A tractor?'

Charlie blushed beetroot red as she climbed down from the passenger seat. There hadn't been any time to get changed, so she was still wearing her jodhpurs. As she ran across the car park, the moos started.

First it was one, then a couple, then it seemed like the whole school was mooing like a herd of cows desperate to be milked.

Tears pricked Charlie's eyes as she joined her class, where Vanessa Veasey was mooing loudest of all. She wished the ground would open up and swallow her whole.

Suddenly a voice bellowed, 'Enough!'

It was Harry, stepping out of line and turning to face the whole school.

'That's our sister you're having a go at, and it's not fair. She's cleverer and stronger and works harder than all of you lot put together. So just stop it, *right now*.'

'Yeah!' Larry added, joining his brother. 'And if any of you think you're better than us because you've never milked a cow, or mucked out a stable, or ridden in a cattle truck – well, I've got news for you: you might smell a bit fresher, but you're not better.'

The mooing stopped and the bullies responsible shifted on their feet.

Polly hurried up to Charlie and gave her a fierce hug.

'What's got into your brothers?'

'No idea,' said Charlie, smiling as she wiped her nose. 'I think Noble Warrior must have magic powers because they've changed. I'm not sure I recognize them, but I certainly like them a whole lot more!'

Chapter 10

Even Boris wasn't awake when the rest of the house started moving. It was the day of the race at Salisbury and everyone knew what they needed to do. If they'd forgotten, they only had to look at the timetable Charlie had stuck on the wall next to the back door.

5 a.m.: Joe and Harry milk cows.
5.30 a.m.: Dad wash cattle truck.

Charlie and Larry lead out Noble Warrior and Percy. Clean tack, plait manes, oil hooves.

6 a.m.: Mum feed pigs, chickens and Boris. Make picnic for journey (no cake!).

6.30 a.m.: Breakfast.

7 a.m.: Leave for Salisbury.

Charlie gave Noble Warrior a small feed that morning and encouraged him to drink a little bit of water.

'You mustn't have too much,' she explained as he turned his big head towards her. 'You won't be able to gallop if you've got a bucket of water swilling around in your tummy.'

She pulled his ears and kissed him on the soft bit of his muzzle. She could feel butterflies in her stomach. 'You're going to be a racehorse today. A real racehorse.'

As Charlie headed back into the house, she heard her parents talking in the kitchen. She paused at the door, not wanting to interrupt them.

'I've written the bank a letter,' her mum was saying. 'They've agreed to extend the overdraft, but only if we start repaying it in the next two months. If we don't, the bank will make us sell the farm.'

'They can't do that!' said Mr Bass.

'They can, darling. And they will.'

Charlie's heart sank. Sell Folly Farm? Where would they go? She couldn't imagine her family in one of the trendy flats in town.

'There might be one solution,' said Mr Bass reluctantly. 'We always said Noble Warrior was a business investment. Everyone understood, including Charlie. If we get an offer to buy him, we've got to take it. This might come down to the farm or the horse. I'm not sure we can afford to keep both.'

After breakfast, the family piled into the cattle truck. Charlie was very quiet. After what her parents had said, she couldn't face trying to be jolly with her brothers and, besides, there wasn't room.

'Move your bum a bit, Larry – you're sitting on the handbrake.'

Mr Bass shoved the gear stick into first and they rumbled down the drive. Charlie tried singing quietly to herself, to keep the nerves at bay and try and forget what she had heard.

Six hours later, she didn't have the energy or the voice to sing. Instead, she had tears streaming down her face.

Most athletes will say that they learn more from their defeats than from their victories. They will always 'find the positives', even in a situation that seems to be nothing but negative. Charlie did her best to think like this, but, try as she might, she couldn't come up with a bright side.

They had laughed. The crowd had actually laughed as Percy led Noble Warrior into the paddock. Then Bryan Dennis had come up with a face like thunder.

'What do you think this is, a blinking circus? I'm the champion jockey. I don't need to be trailing round after a podgy pony. Get him out of here!'

Charlie had tried to tell him that it would be a mistake, but he didn't listen. Then Noble Warrior got upset and started dancing on the spot and, when Mr Bass tried to give Bryan Dennis a leg-up, his tweed suit wouldn't let him reach high enough and Bryan Dennis ended up in the grass.

There was no upside to that at all.

And it went downhill from there. Noble Warrior planted himself on the racecourse and refused to canter down to the start, so Bryan Dennis had taken his whip and given him three sharp cracks on the backside. Charlie's father looked horrified, but it was her mother who had reacted the most surprisingly. Mrs Bass had sprinted across the lawn in front of the grandstand to accost the champion jockey.

'I'll have that!' she'd shouted, snatching his whip. 'Don't you dare hit my daughter's horse, you mean little man!'

Charlie remembered the look of fury on her mother's face. She was proud of her, especially considering she wasn't a natural horsewoman. She had never been as close to Noble Warrior as the rest

of the family and, to be honest, Charlie hadn't realized how much she cared.

'Let me lead you,' Charlie had said to Bryan Dennis. 'We might be able to get him to the start if I run with you, but it'll take a while . . .'

They eventually arrived at the start with Noble Warrior in a muck lather of sweat, and Bryan Dennis in a sullen, silent mood.

With Percy nowhere to be seen, Noble Warrior was disorientated. A team of stalls handlers were around him, pulling him forward and pushing from behind. He didn't like it and once again planted himself firmly on the spot. He wouldn't budge forwards, backwards or sideways. Bryan Dennis lifted his arm to smack him again before he'd realized he didn't have a whip any more.

'It might be best if I took over,' Charlie had said quietly. She led Noble Warrior forward into his narrow starting stall and kissed him on the nose.

As she ducked under the gate, though, Charlie suddenly realized that, for all the fitness work they had done with Noble Warrior, he'd never started out of stalls before. So it wasn't surprising that, when the gates opened and all the other horses leaped forward, he just stood there. Bryan Dennis had growled and shouted and kicked, but he wouldn't budge.

'Go on, Noddy!' Charlie had clicked at him from the sidelines. 'Canter on and we'll see you at the finish.'

Looking back, she had to laugh at the thought of the helpless champion jockey on a horse who refused to run. It didn't matter what she said or what Bryan Dennis tried to do: Noble Warrior would not budge. The rest of the horses galloped away and he just stood there. Bryan Dennis dismounted while he was still in the stalls and got a lift back to the weighing room in the ambulance.

'Thanks for making me a laughing stock,' he spluttered at Charlie as it drove off. 'I'll leave you to get that useless donkey out of here.'

It took Charlie ten minutes of gentle coaxing, but eventually Noble Warrior came out of the stalls backwards. The race was long over. Charlie led him back to the paddock while the crowd clapped sarcastically. Some of them laughed again, but others were angry. One man threw a betting slip at her.

'You've cost me ten quid, you have!' he shouted. 'Don't suppose you'll be paying me back, will you?'

As Charlie led Noble Warrior back to the stables, she noticed a sharp-faced man checking him out. When she went back to the weighing room later, to return the number cloth, she'd seen him in conversation with Bryan Dennis.

'Do you think they'd sell?' the man was asking.

'He might look handsome,' the jockey replied, 'but I'm telling you: don't touch him.'

Back in the cattle truck, Charlie cried into Noble Warrior's mane.

'Oh, Noddy,' she said. 'I know you didn't mean to mess everything up, but now no one will want to buy you. There's only one way out of this. We just have to win the Derby.'

Charlie took a deep breath. There was so much to do. They needed to see if they could get permission from the Senior Steward at Epsom for Percy to accompany Noble Warrior in the paddock and on the way to the start. They needed a new headcollar, rope and paddock sheet so that he didn't look as if he'd just come off the farm. Joe needed to get his jockey's licence because it was clear that, after the embarrassment at Salisbury, no one else would be willing to ride. Finally, they needed to work out a way of getting Percy from the start of the Derby to the finish before Noble Warrior.

There was plenty to ponder.

Before the cattle truck crossed the border into Hampshire, Charlie had stopped crying. When they were ten miles from home, she had started planning. And, by the time she was thrown sideways by the potholes of Folly Farm, she honestly saw no reason why Noble Warrior couldn't win the Derby.

'And that's another thing we could do with the prize money,' she muttered to herself. 'Get this drive resurfaced.'

Chapter 11

Two days later, a letter arrived from the British Racing School addressed to Joe Butler Esq.

Mrs Bass put it on Joe's plate and, when he'd peeled off his overalls and sat down for breakfast, the whole family looked at him.

Joe didn't move. He just sat there, staring at the envelope.

'Open it!' said Harry and Larry together.

'I can't,' said Joe. 'What if it's bad news and I haven't passed and I can't get a licence and I can't ride Noddy in the Derby? What then?'

Charlie leaned over to put an arm round his shoulder.

'Well,' she said, 'we won't know unless you open it, will we?'

Joe nodded and opened the envelope. Inside was a letter and, from between the folds, a certificate fell on to the table. Slowly, Joe turned it over to reveal . . . a jockey's licence!

The Basses cheered.

Joseph Michael Butler was now officially a jockey. With that one piece of paper, he could ride any horse in any race anywhere in the country.

'Your dad would be really proud,' said Charlie.

Joe swallowed hard and looked down at Boris, who was curled round his feet.

'Yes, I think he would be. But I know exactly what he'd say now. "Make sure you prepare, lad.

Watch everything, read everything, think of everything." He was a perfectionist, my dad.'

Joe took a mouthful of tea and thought for a minute. 'Harry, can you do me a favour? Dig out as many YouTube videos of the Derby as you can find. Not just the race, all the build-up as well. The paddock, the parade in front of the stands, the canter down to the start, everything.'

'No problem,' said Harry. 'I'll have it ready by this afternoon.'

'Do you really think we can do it?' asked Mrs Bass. 'Only one horse in over two hundred years has managed to win the Derby without ever running before.'

'They had an article about him in the paper the other day,' said Joe. 'He was called Amato. He never ran before the Derby and never ran again after. They say his coat was so white everyone thought he was a ghost.'

'I saw that too,' said Larry. 'There's a pub in Epsom named after him now and the night before the Derby a name appears above the well, written

162

in chalk. They say it's the fairies' prediction of who'll win.'

Charlie wasn't listening.

'I think we need to try galloping him backwards,' she said.

'Backwards?' Mr Bass asked, looking at her as if she'd lost her marbles.

'Yes. Backwards on the gallop. We always go *up* the hill. I think we need to come down it a few times, so Noddy can work out where to put his legs and doesn't panic when he comes down the hill at Epsom. It would also be good if we could turn him left at the bottom of the hill, just like it will be at Tattenham Corner.'

'OK,' said Joe. 'Let's give it a go.'

Charlie and Percy left Joe at the top of the hill as they cantered slowly down. Charlie's riding had improved beyond all recognition, but she still didn't enjoy the sensation of going downhill. Her position in the saddle felt all wrong and she didn't know whether to put her legs forwards or backwards.

Percy was far too enthusiastic because downhill was also the way home. He started to gather pace.

'Whoa, boy. Steady there.' Charlie tried to keep her voice calm as she set her weight against the reins to slow him down. Percy ignored her.

As they thundered down the hill, Charlie swung all her weight on to her left side to try and steer Percy round the corner.

'Come on, legs. You can do this,' she said. 'Like Mum said: Serena Williams has got powerful legs. Beyoncé has got powerful legs. This is what they're for!'

She used all her strength to wheel Percy round to the left so he was heading along the bottom of the field and then back up the hill. Finally, he slowed down.

'I know exactly what you were thinking, you greedy thing,' she scolded him. 'That if you got back to the barn first, you could guzzle all the hay before Noddy got there. Weren't you?'

Percy turned his blue eye towards her and closed it briefly.

'Don't you wink at me! That was terrifying. You are the naughtiest pony in the world and you don't deserve all the love you get.'

Percy looked so miserable at her stern words that Charlie had to laugh.

'Right, you stand still and let's watch Noddy come down the hill.'

Noble Warrior looked a little uncertain as he set off and Joe kept him in a steady canter. Gradually, he seemed to find his feet, though, and, as they cornered smoothly at the bottom, Charlie noticed that his front left leg was striking the ground first, which was exactly what needed to happen.

'That looks great!' she shouted to Joe. 'He's leading on the left leg.'

Joe puffed out his cheeks as he pulled up alongside her.

'It's not much fun, cantering downhill,' he said. 'But I think we need to do it a few more times.'

He patted Noble Warrior on the neck. 'This fella's got such good balance it doesn't really bother him. I'm the one who needs to practise. I don't want to fall off coming round Tattenham Corner. That would be embarrassing.'

'You just need to get the angle right,' Charlie said, thinking about the maths lesson on angles and tangents she'd had that week. 'That's the key . . .'

'Joe,' said Charlie later that afternoon, after they'd watched a YouTube clip of Shergar winning the Derby in 1981. 'Have a look at this diagram. I've been studying the layout of Epsom Downs. You know that from the mile-and-a-half start the course goes uphill to a height of a hundred and fifty-three metres above sea level, then comes steeply downhill and left round Tattenham Corner? The drop is about the same as seven double-decker buses.'

Joe nodded, looking at the detailed map Charlie had drawn. It showed a line coming off the apex of the bend.

'Well, I think I've worked out the optimum angle of delivery from Tattenham Corner into the straight.'

Joe looked at her sideways.

'What's that mean in English?'

'It means there's no point hugging the rail,' Charlie explained. 'That might look like the shortest way, but because the ground is on a slope it throws you off balance. You want to be at least four horse-widths off the rail. There's a strip of ground that's known as the Golden Highway.'

Joe sucked in his breath.

'If you get on that strip,' continued Charlie, 'Noddy will be able to gallop straight to the finish. Hold him together down the hill and round the bend, then, when you reach the two-furlong marker, you can let him go.'

Charlie had seen this happen with a couple of horses on YouTube. One called Lammtarra had come flying from the back of the field to pass everyone else and win. Maybe his jockey had found the Golden Highway.

To get to the finish with a chance, Charlie knew they had to improve Noble Warrior's start. At Salisbury, he wouldn't come out of the starting stalls at all. At Epsom, he needed to jump out and gallop as soon as the front gates opened.

Luckily, Larry had an idea. First he built up two walls of straw bales with a narrow gap between them, just wide enough for a horse to squeeze in. Then he added a couple of sheep hurdles that could be pulled open by a piece of baler twine on either side.

They started by walking Percy through the gap with Noble Warrior following behind him. Then Joe made Noddy stand in the 'stall' for a few minutes before walking on through. Next they shut the sheep-hurdle gates and made him wait in the stall for a few moments before opening them. He trotted out. Finally, Charlie took Percy a hundred metres away and, when Harry and Larry pulled the string to open the gates, Noble Warrior shot out and galloped towards them.

'Good boy,' said Joe, patting him on the neck. 'That's more like it!'

Every day, they practised in the bale stall, adding extra elements. They banged pots and pans so that Noddy could get used to loud noises and wouldn't be

put off if another horse started kicking or rattling the starting stalls. They played loud music on the radio to echo the sound of Epsom on Derby Day, including the noise from the fairground in the middle of the course, which featured rides and dodgem cars.

Noble Warrior was getting better and better at going into the makeshift stall – and at galloping out of it. Eventually, he would even do it when Percy was standing behind him rather than in front. Charlie gave him an extra carrot and a kiss on the nose for that.

'Mum,' said Charlie that evening. 'We need to book the farrier before the Derby. Noddy needs to have racing shoes put on him so he can lift his feet more easily. That way he'll gallop faster. I noticed the horses at Salisbury all had different-looking shoes. Apparently, they're made of aluminium so they're really light.'

'Sounds just like an athlete wearing spikes for a race,' said Mrs Bass. 'I expect they're expensive, are they?'

'I'll call Alex Williams,' said Mr Bass. 'He has his own farrier at Cherrydown and he might let us use him at a reduced cost.'

Harry and Charlie were studying the latest *Racing Post* when the phone rang. It was five days before the Derby and the list of runners had reduced from sixty in May to just eighteen horses. Noble Warrior was one of them. He was still 1,000–1 in the betting, the outsider of the whole field, and Harry was trying to work out how much money they could make on a ten-pound bet.

'I'll get it,' said Charlie, picking up the phone. 'It might be Alex Williams about the farrier. Hello?'

'Hello, love,' said an unfamiliar voice. 'Is Bill Bass there?'

'He's out in the yard,' replied Charlie. 'Madonna's got a wart on her udder and he's trying to treat it.'

'Madonna? What's she doing on your farm?'

'Oh, she's been here for years. She can be grumpy if you don't treat her properly, but she produces lots of milk.'

Charlie could hear scratching on the other end of the line. She thought the man might be writing down what she was saying.

'I can ask my dad to ring you back. Who shall I say called?'

'That would be great. It's Piers Cleverly. I'm the racing correspondent for the *Moon*. You've probably heard of me. I'm known as "The Ace From Outer Space". I've picked the last three Derby winners. I always do a feature on the horse I think will win, plus one on a rank outsider with no chance. So I'd like to talk to your dad about Noble Warrior.'

'Smart move,' said Charlie. 'If you want to pick the winner again, you should.'

'Not as my winning tip,' laughed the man. 'He's my hopeless case.'

Charlie decided she didn't like the sound of this journalist at all.

'So, if your horse is going to win the Derby,' Piers Cleverly continued, 'what will you say when you meet the Queen?'

'The Queen?'

'Yes, didn't you know? She's always at the Derby,' said Piers Cleverly, beginning to laugh again. 'So you'd better start practising your curtsey. In case you win!'

Charlie was about to give the reporter a piece of her mind when her dad came in.

'Here's my father now,' she said. 'And you'll be laughing on the other side of your face when Noddy wins.'

She handed the phone to Mr Bass and settled down to listen to her father's conversation.

'How did we get into racing? Well, we decided it was a better idea than *Strictly Come Chicken Dancing*. My daughter? Yes, she can ride. She learned on one of the cows. The cattle truck? Oh, I've had that since 1985. Not much to look at, but it'll get to Epsom just fine, don't you worry.'

Her father was laughing away as he spoke, but Charlie felt uneasy, especially when she heard her father agree to send Piers Cleverly a photograph of the family on the farm. She had a nagging suspicion that the journalist was up to something.

Three days later, when Joe brought in a copy of the *Moon*, she realized she'd been right. Dad's photo was on the front page, under the headline:

Fruitcake Farmer Dreams of Derby Success

Inside was a double-page spread by Piers Cleverly. Mr Bass read the article slowly and, as he did so, his cheeks started to turn bright red.

'He's made me sound like a complete idiot!'

'Well, to be fair,' said Mrs Bass, 'you sometimes *are* a bit of an idiot. But you're *my* idiot. How dare he? Give me that paper.'

She scanned the article in under a minute, noticing five spelling mistakes, ten incorrect uses of punctuation and thirty-six factual errors.

'Leave it with me,' she said, disappearing to her office to compose an email to the editor of the *Moon* demanding a full apology.

After that, Mr Bass refused to talk to any more journalists. He even turned down the local TV station, despite the fact that his favourite sports reporter, Daisy Destiny, wanted to do a special report.

'Best to stay under the radar,' Mrs Bass agreed. 'No point in drawing any more attention to ourselves.'

One unexpected benefit of the article, though, was that Mr Bass had told Piers Cleverly that Mrs Bass didn't have anything suitable to wear to the Derby. The next day, Polly's mum came to the rescue again, bringing over a selection of three designer outfits and matching hats for Caroline to choose from. She also brought Mr Williams's morning suit and top hat for Mr Bass to try on.

Although the jacket was a bit long and the trousers too tight, it was far better than his itchy tweed suit.

'I just don't know what I'd do without you, Jasmine,' said Mrs Bass, hugging her.

'That's what friends are for,' replied Mrs Williams, climbing back into her car. 'By the way, Alex said to tell you that he'll be sending over his farrier in the horsebox. He says you can take it for the day. We'll look after Boris and we'll all be watching on TV, cheering you on. Good luck!' she shouted through the window as she glided away down the drive.

'Such a nice woman,' said Mrs Bass. 'And to think I felt so intimidated when I first met her because she was wearing smart clothes and I wasn't. Ridiculous.'

Chapter 12

The night before the Derby, Charlie couldn't sleep. She lay in bed with Boris, thinking about all the things that might go wrong. Eventually, she decided to get up. There was no point tossing and turning if she could do something more useful.

She and Boris crept downstairs, just as they had done the first night Noble Warrior and Percy had come to Folly Farm, and went out to the barn. The racehorse and the palomino pony were lying down together. Percy had the midnight munchies and was filling the hole in his tummy by tucking into his bed of straw.

'You shouldn't eat that, Percy. It's bad for your digestion,' whispered Charlie as she sat down cross-legged and leaned back on to Percy's tummy. He turned his head to have a quick frisk of her pockets in case there was a treat lurking there. Noble Warrior rested his head on her knee, his ears flickering backwards and forwards.

'Big day tomorrow, Noddy, but it'll all be OK. I'll be with you at the start and Joe will be riding you this time, so you'll always have a friend right there. Percy and I can't keep up with you once you set off, so you'll just have to trust me that we're not going far. We're going to cut across the middle of the course, through the fairground, so you'll meet us at the finish two and a half minutes later. Does that sound OK?'

Noddy made a noise that sounded like some sort of agreement. Charlie felt better about things now that she'd explained her plan. She hadn't told anyone else about it. Not her parents, not the boys, not even Joe, because she was worried they might try to stop her, or let it slip to someone official and she'd be banned from going to the start at all.

Charlie snuggled down into the straw and put her head in the warm, soft spot between Percy's tummy and his front leg. And that's where Joe found her the next morning when he arrived to milk the cows.

'Hey, Boris, whatcha doing out here, fella? Got your mistress here too, have you?'

Charlie stretched and yawned. She might not have had a mattress or a duvet, but she couldn't fault a bed of straw for comfort. Boris got up and wagged his tail at Joe, then ran back to lick Charlie on the face.

'Morning, Charlie! Rise and shine. It's Derby Day!'

'Morning, Joe. How are you feeling?'

'Ah, you know, it's a huge day, but I reckon it's best to just focus on one thing at a time. So milking, here I come, and we'll worry about the rest when it happens.'

Listening to Joe, Charlie thought about what she had read in *How to Find the Olympian Within*. All champions had talent and worked hard, but what set the best apart from the rest was their mental approach. They believed in their ability and they had to be able to focus and think calmly under pressure. She knew Joe could do that. It might be Derby Day and he might be about to ride against the champion jockey, Bryan Dennis, the Irish champion, Fingal O'Connor, and the French champion, Thierry Goujon, but he would do what he always did – work hard, keep his concentration and try his best, whether he was milking the cows or riding Noble Warrior.

A few moments later, Harry appeared to check that Joe and Charlie were sticking to the timetable. He had picked a handful of sweet clover and offered it to Noble Warrior. As he stroked his nose and watched him munching it, he noticed something.

'Hey, that one's got four leaves!'

Harry thrust his hand towards Noble Warrior's muzzle, but he was a second too late. The four-leafed clover got sucked into his mouth and disappeared.

'Argh! That was a four-leafed clover! I saw it as clear as day and I've never found one before. It might have made all the difference today.'

'Well, it hasn't really gone anywhere,' reasoned Charlie. 'It's inside Noddy's tummy, so maybe that means he'll have all the luck.'

Charlie stroked Noble Warrior's lean stomach.

'Let's hope it works,' she said. 'Because we can plan all we like, but we'll still need a bit of luck to win the Derby. Oh, Noddy, please be a good boy today.'

At six o'clock on the dot, the huge black-and-gold Cherrydown horsebox rumbled into the farmyard. Charlie and Joe were going to travel with the horses and the farrier while the rest of the family followed in the jeep.

'This isn't a horsebox,' exclaimed Charlie as they set off. 'It's a hotel on wheels!'

The Cherrydown horsebox had running water, a sleeping area and a TV. She could even sit in the back, comfortably near the horses, and still talk to Joe through a sliding door to the front cab.

'There's so much room back here and you can't even hear the engine or feel the ruts when you're driving. I don't think Noddy even knows we're moving.'

'Look what I've found,' said Joe, holding up a bag with a note on it. 'It's from Alex Williams. It says: "Just a few things you might need today. Good luck!"'

Inside the bag was a pair of paper-thin white breeches along with some boots made of soft leather. There was also a shiny patent saddle with titanium stirrups that Charlie guessed weighed less than a kilogram, and a racing bridle with the cheekpieces and reins stitched on to the bit so that they couldn't break mid-race. Everything was designed to be hard-wearing and practical, but as light as a feather.

The journey to Epsom was smoother and faster than it ever had been in the cattle truck and at 10.30 they turned into the entrance that said RACECOURSE STABLES.

Mr Bass may have turned down all press requests since Piers Cleverly had made fun of him in the *Moon*, but he couldn't avoid them at the racecourse. The TV cameras were there as the horsebox drove in, and the producer recognized him at the wheel of the battered old jeep following behind the horsebox.

They filmed the ramp coming down before Charlie led Percy down it, followed by Joe leading Noble Warrior. Percy veered off towards the nearest camera, dragging Charlie with him. He made a lunge for the big furry microphone, biting a lump out of it.

'Oi!' shouted the sound operator. 'That's thousands of pounds' worth of damage, you little blighter!'

Percy turned his back and lined up his hooves.

'Watch out!' shouted Charlie. 'He kicks.'

But, with his usual bad behaviour, Percy had actually created the perfect distraction. While the camera crew fussed over their damaged equipment, Noble Warrior walked calmly into the seclusion of the stables, unnoticed and unfilmed. Harry and Larry agreed to stay with the horses while their parents went to double-check the permissions they had requested to allow Percy into the paddock and down to the start.

Joe and Charlie headed off to do the most important prep of all – walking the course. The area in the middle was already busy with families who had arrived early to enjoy the build-up. Charlie could see a line of open-topped double-decker buses coming in from the main road and making their way down the inside rail to park up along the final two furlongs. Some were already in position, with people on the top deck drinking champagne.

There were fairground rides, a stage with singers on it, fortune-tellers, bookmakers, ice-cream sellers and thousands of cars with families having picnics. Some people had already put rugs down to save their places on Tattenham Corner so they'd be in the right place for the Derby five hours later.

'It's a giant party!' said Charlie. 'I thought Harry and Larry were overdoing it when they kept playing all that loud music to Noddy while we were training, but they were right.'

Charlie and Joe walked together for a mile and a half until they reached the end of the white rails that marked out the racecourse. A red-and-white marker read DERBY START, and from there they looked back towards the grandstand.

'So this is it,' said Charlie. 'The most famous race in the world and the most difficult racecourse.'

'You've done all the work to get Noddy here,' said Joe. 'You bought him in the first place and, if it wasn't for you and Percy, we wouldn't have been able to get him fit. Now I've got to make sure I don't let you down.'

'You would never do that,' said Charlie.

She could see that Joe was in race mode and wanted time on his own to think through his tactics. And she was happy to leave him to it because she had a different route to plan . . .

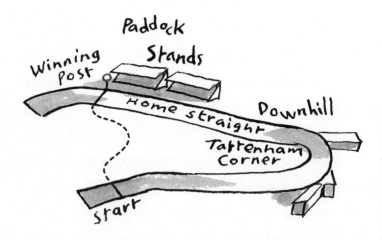

The Derby course was a horseshoe shape so, as the crow flies, the start was only a quarter of a mile from the finish. Charlie knew that if she could work out a route that was safe and fast, she and Percy could get to the winning post before Noble Warrior did. She had to find a position where he could see Percy because when he spotted his little friend ahead of him Noddy would kick into turbo charge and then *anything* was possible.

Picking up a dusty path across the common ground in the middle of the course, Charlie followed it through some scrubland and past a collection of caravans.

An old lady with jet-black hair, a hook nose and wrinkles on her face was sitting on a stool in front of a table. She was playing with a pack of cards.

'All right, my lovely?' she called as Charlie walked past.

'Fine, thank you,' replied Charlie. She smiled and the woman smiled back. She had gaps in her mouth where teeth were missing.

'Come 'ere, my love. I can feel your winning power. You are a champion, my love, and you will be an even greater champion by the end of today.'

Charlie wasn't sure what to do. She needed to work out the route to the finish and then get back to the stables to check on Noble Warrior, but she didn't want to be rude. Besides, she was intrigued by the old woman's words.

As if by magic, the old lady produced a stool for Charlie to sit on. She patted it and said, 'Come on, my love, 'ave your cards read. I'm a Romany traveller, a direct descendant of Gypsy Rose Lee, the finest fortune-teller that ever there was, and there's no one but me who will give you a true reading.'

A fortune-teller! Charlie couldn't resist. She sat on the stool and the old woman started to shuffle the cards.

'I'll deal you three cards, my love. Just three cards and we'll see what lies in store for you.'

She turned over the first card. It was a circle, like a compass with strange Egyptian-looking symbols on the outer side of the circle.

'You shall be lucky today, my dear. The Wheel of Fortune is on your side. Now, what else do the cards have for you?'

She turned over the second card to reveal a man in a chariot.

'Aha, the Chariot. For strength and victory. You will be lucky and you will be victorious. This is a good day for you, a good day indeed.'

Charlie leaned further forward and waited for the third card. As it flipped over, she heard the fortune-teller suck in her breath. The card showed a woman with flowing blonde hair sitting on a throne.

'It's the Empress, the card of royalty, creativity and power. What you believe in will happen. Today is your day.'

Charlie's head was spinning. If only it could be true!

'Now, before you go, my love,' continued the fortune-teller, 'that'll be twenty pounds, please. I'm giving you a discount on account of your age. I'm sure you'll agree it's worth it.'

'Well,' said Charlie, 'those cards are certainly worth twenty pounds. I think they mean we're going to win the Derby and I will meet the Queen.'

'Win the Derby? What with, my lovely, what with?' asked the old woman. 'What's the name of the horse?'

'Well, I would tell you,' said Charlie, 'but I'm afraid it's expensive information.'

The fortune-teller smiled her toothless smile.

'And how much will it cost me, my little friend?' she asked.

'Oh, twenty pounds – and I'm giving you a discount on account of you being so generous to me.'

'Ha ha ha!' cackled the old woman. 'You're a canny one, my dear. You'll go far, my love, you'll go far. I've not seen cards that good all day and I'm willing to take a chance. Deal.'

She spat on her hand and held it out. Charlie shook it, feeling the roughness of her skin.

'Noble Warrior is the horse,' she said. 'He'll be a thousand to one or thereabouts.'

The fortune-teller's eyes widened. 'I've heard that name! It's the very one that appeared on the well at the Amato last night. Everyone was talking about it. They all said the fairies must have gone mad, picking a thousand-to-one outsider, but they're on your side and so are the cards. Good luck, my girl!'

Charlie left the fortune-teller laughing to herself and carried on down the hill towards the finish line. She felt a new confidence blossoming inside her. If she got her plan right and stayed calm enough to carry it out, she knew she could save the farm. But everything hinged on getting from the start to the finish line in less than two minutes. She had to get across the centre of the racecourse, past the caravans where the fortune-teller lived and round the edge of the fairground.

As she approached the finish line, Charlie could see a tiny gap in the rail with a security man guarding the gate.

'Morning, miss,' he said as Charlie approached. 'Could I see your pass, please?'

Charlie showed him her laminated pass.

'Bit young to be a trainer, aren't you?'

'I'm the youngest trainer ever to have a runner in the Derby,' Charlie confirmed.

'Oh, I know who you are!' said the guard with a flash of recognition. 'You're one of that mad farming lot, the ones with the horse who doesn't gallop.'

'He does now,' said Charlie. 'And, if I were you, I'd put a bet on at a thousand to one while you still can. If you would please let me through this gate on my pony, Percy, at exactly two minutes past four this afternoon, I promise you it will make all the difference.'

'Will it indeed?' The security guard stood up to his full height. 'Well, seeing as you're the politest trainer I've come across, I will. Good luck to you, miss!'

As Charlie passed through the gate, she spotted Joe walking the last furlong of the course.

'You were right!' he beamed, running over to her. 'There's no point going near the inside rail because the ground slopes into it, and we'd be off balance, so I've picked a flag on the end of the grandstand that I can aim for. That'll be my line.'

'Excellent,' said Charlie as they walked towards the grandstand. 'And I've found a good route through the middle of the common so I can hopefully get to the finish line before you do. By the way, did you hear about the name above the well at the Amato?'

Joe shook his head.

'Well, I made a friend in the fairground and she told me that the name that appeared in chalk was Noble Warrior!'

'Really?' said Joe. 'Well, I never.'

'Look, there's the winner's enclosure,' exclaimed Charlie, pointing towards a small circular area beside the course.

As she did so, a small man barged past them. It was Bryan Dennis.

'Enjoy the view,' he sneered, 'because this is as close as you'll get to it. And make sure you keep well out of my way,' he snarled at Joe.

A taller man, in jockey's breeches and a light jacket, was running out of the weighing room towards the course. Charlie recognized him as Fingal O'Connor, the Irish champion jockey.

'Pay no attention to that grumpy old so-and-so,' he said as he came past them. 'I could see him having a go at you. He's only nervous because he's on the favourite and everyone will think him a fool if he gets beaten. You're lucky. No one's expecting you to win – apart from those fairies at the Amato, so I hear!'

'Thanks,' said Joe. 'We hope they're right! Well, I'll see you later, Charlie.'

Taking a deep breath, he turned and disappeared into the area reserved for jockeys only.

Charlie took another look at the winner's enclosure. It was tiny. At most courses, there would have been space for the second, third and fourth placed horses alongside the winner, but at Epsom only the winner was allowed to come into this small white-fenced circle.

Just then, her parents appeared.

'We've got all the permissions confirmed,' said her dad. 'You can ride Percy into the paddock and down to the start as long as you promise to make your own way back and not get in anyone's way.'

'I promise,' said Charlie, feeling her face flush. Her plan to cross the middle of the racecourse wasn't *exactly* not getting in anyone's way. But she knew she had to take risks if she was going to save the farm.

'We've all been invited to a drinks reception for the owners and trainers,' said Mrs Bass. 'I thought we'd leave the boys to oversee things in the stables, but maybe you'd like to come, just to take your mind off things?'

Charlie couldn't think of anything she'd less like to go to than a grown-ups' drinks reception.

'No thanks, Mum. I'll go back to the stables and check on Noddy. You go and enjoy yourselves.'

As she headed towards the stables, Charlie picked up a copy of the racecard. Sitting outside Noble Warrior's stable on a bale of hay, she looked through the Derby field. There were comments beside each runner. For Noble Warrior, it said:

'Refused to start at Salisbury in only race.' After the text was a squiggle.

'Harry,' she said, 'what does this mean?'

'Ah, the infamous squiggle,' Harry grinned. 'They give that to lots of horses – don't worry. It just means they don't really know what to expect from them.'

Charlie checked Noble Warrior over and brushed him until every hair was perfectly straight. She put a tiny bit of baby oil on the brush to give his tail extra shine.

An hour later, her parents reappeared and Charlie immediately noticed her mother's hat was sitting at a strange angle.

'Have you been drinking champagne, Mum?'

'Of course not,' her mother replied with a tiny hiccup.

Mr Bass raised his eyebrows.

'Why don't you have a little sit-down?' asked Larry, helping his mother towards a bale of straw.

Mrs Bass sat wonkily and shut her eyes.

Charlie looked at her watch. It was half past two. According to Harry's schedule for the day, she was due to get the saddle from Joe in the weighing room at three o'clock, so she headed off along the rubbery track towards the parade ring, turned right at the top and through the back door.

As Charlie went in, there was a bubble of commentary from the public address system, rising to a crescendo, blending in with the cheers of the crowd as the runners of one of the early races reached the winning post. Through the tinted windows of the weighing room, she glimpsed a flash of colours. She couldn't tell who had won. Most of the other trainers and jockeys with runners in the Derby had horses in the earlier races as well. They were busy all day long, while Charlie and Joe only had one race to worry about.

Joe came out of the changing room with a tiny saddle under his arm, the girths wrapped round it. He looked dapper in his racing silks and brand-new white breeches. Charlie sucked in her breath as she took in the green-and-gold jacket he was wearing and the gold cap Joe was holding over the top of the saddle.

He stepped up on to the scales and the weight appeared on a huge digital display on the wall. A round man with grey hair sat behind a desk and said sharply to Joe: 'Number 12 for the Derby?'

'Yes, sir,' said Joe.

'Green with gold braid and a gold cap,' said the round man, confirming Joe's colours. 'Nine stone exactly.'

The door burst open and several jockeys marched through.

'Out of my way,' said a surly voice. It was Bryan Dennis. He nearly knocked Joe to the floor as he barged him off the scales and then stomped off into the changing room.

'Did he just get beaten?' Charlie asked the next jockey in line.

'No, he won,' replied the jockey. 'Doesn't matter if he wins or loses, he's always a misery!'

Joe handed his saddle to Charlie over the rail.

'How's Noddy?' he asked.

'He's settled in really well,' said Charlie. 'The boys are taking him and Percy for a walk now because that's what Seamus O'Reilly's lads are doing with his runners.'

'I've hated being away from you all,' said Joe. 'I've been trying to ask some of the older jockeys about riding in the Derby, but they've all been coming and going, riding in races, and in between they don't say much.'

'You don't need their advice anyway,' replied Charlie. 'You know what you have to do. Now, I'd better get back.'

Charlie gave Joe an encouraging smile and headed down to the stables. It was over half a mile away and the change of atmosphere was extreme. Up in the grandstand, there was a buzz, like electricity being passed from person to person. There were colourful hats and men in tailcoats, there was shouting and the clinking of glasses. Down in the stables, there was only the *clip-clop* of hooves and the steady slosh of water as runners from the race before were hosed down.

It'll be much better to saddle Noddy here in the calm, she thought. *He won't be so worried.*

Harry and Larry looked exhausted. They had been walking Percy and Noble Warrior round and round in a large circle for half an hour.

'Let's saddle them up!' Charlie suggested. Her brothers' faces lit up as they hurried back towards the boxes.

'I can't believe you're flagging already,' she said to them as she carefully put the number cloth and saddle on Noble Warrior. 'If you worked for Seamus O'Reilly, you'd have to lead your horse for four miles every day, so by the time you'd ridden three horses you'd also have walked twelve miles.'

'Huh,' said Harry. 'Well, good for them. Anyway, we don't work for Seamus O'Reilly, we work for you.'

'That's right,' said Larry. 'You're our guv'nor.'

Charlie was still getting used to this change in attitude. What had happened to the boys who called her 'Thunder Thighs' and tried to push her into the electric fence and told her she couldn't play with them?

'Glad to see you lads have finally seen sense,' said their mother, who had just woken up. She sat up and straightened her hat. 'Right, what are we waiting for? We've got a Derby to win!'

'Let's go,' said Charlie, before leaning in to whisper in Noble Warrior's ear. 'There'll be a lot of noise and a lot of fuss and a lot of horses and people who think they're better than us, but I want you to know one thing – no horse is better than you. You can gallop if you want to and today would be a very good day to want that. No planting yourself in the stalls, no rearing up or refusing to budge. Just be the best you can be. Whatever happens, I love you.'

Noble Warrior flicked his ears backwards and forwards. Charlie hoped he understood. She walked into Percy's box to find him in a sulk because he had been ignored. He pinned his ears flat back and bared his teeth at her.

'Oh, come on, Percy, you look like Bryan Dennis! This is a big day for you too, and you're going to have to be on your best behaviour.'

She put on the riding hat that Polly had lent her, placed her left foot in the stirrup and swung easily into the saddle.

'Come on, team,' she said. 'Time for action.'

Chapter 13

The Bass family entered the parade ring together. Mr and Mrs Bass walked to the centre to wait for Joe, while Charlie led the way on Percy round the outside track. Leaning over the rails were thousands of people. Some were in suits, some in top hat and tails. All the women were wearing bright colours and some of the hats looked good enough to eat. Charlie wasn't the only one who thought so.

'No, Percy, don't!' she said as she tried to pull his head back. She was too late. A bunch of grapes hung from his lips and she saw a woman grasp at her hat, screaming that it had been ruined.

'I'm so sorry!' Charlie shouted over her shoulder. She couldn't exactly stop and offer to replace it, so she decided she could only carry on.

As Percy and Noble Warrior made their first circuit of the ring, Charlie heard the comments of those watching.

'Look, Ma, there's a little one running!'

'Can I bet on the yellow one?'

'Look at his blue eye!'

'I like the look of that Number 12. He's been backed in from a thousand to one to five hundred to one.'

Charlie cocked her head towards the man who'd made that comment.

That's interesting, she thought. *Maybe my fortune-teller has told some other people to have a flutter on him.*

Charlie looked round to see how Noble Warrior was taking it all in. His eyes were bulging and he looked a little surprised, but he wasn't sweating and he wasn't jig-jogging like the French runner, Encore du Vin, who was dripping with sweat.

She saw Seamus O'Reilly saddling his five runners one by one in the centre of the parade ring. He left Little Lion Man, who had won the Derby Trial in Ireland, until last. He was a small horse, not particularly impressive to look at, but Charlie suspected he would be nimble and quick round the corners.

Seamus caught her eye as she rode by and smiled. Then she saw him look at Noble Warrior and nod his approval.

There was a murmur through the crowd and Charlie was told to stop as a group of people entered the parade ring. Percy took advantage of the break in proceedings to empty his bladder. Charlie stood up in the saddle as thick yellow urine flowed forth on to the rubbery path, foaming as it spread rapidly towards the new arrivals.

'Oops,' said a familiar voice. 'Someone was in need.'

Charlie stared. It couldn't be, could it? A small neat figure in a purple dress coat and matching hat was stepping over Percy's pee as she walked into the centre of the parade ring. The woman consulted her racecard as the horses started walking again and looked carefully at Noble Warrior.

'Is that the one I picked?' she asked the man standing next to her.

'That's right, Your Majesty,' he replied. 'Number...'

Charlie strained her ears, but she had moved too far out of earshot to hear any more. Her heart was thumping in her chest. She had totally forgotten that the Queen always came into the parade ring to look at all the runners before the Derby. Joe had told her that they often did a sweepstake in the Royal Box and the Queen would get really excited if she drew the winner. Maybe that's what she meant. Maybe the Queen had got Noble Warrior in the sweepstake. Oh, Charlie hoped so!

Percy had a swagger in his step now that he wasn't so desperate to go to the loo, and marched proudly round the circle.

'You're enjoying this, aren't you?' whispered Charlie, giving him a pat.

Percy gave a little squeal to show his appreciation, but the Canadian hay he had managed to munch in the stables was a bit rich for his digestive system and, as he squealed, he also let off a huge trumpet noise from his bottom. A ripple of laughter spread round the parade ring and Charlie blushed. Why did Percy always have to draw attention to himself? She hoped the Queen hadn't heard it, but, as she passed them again, she saw the royal party in fits of giggles. No such luck.

There was another hold-up for the horses as they made way for the jockeys to come into the parade ring. Charlie saw Bryan Dennis, his face set into a granite-like grimace. She also picked out Thierry Goujon, the French champion jockey, who seemed much smaller than the others. Seamus O'Reilly's five jockeys stood in a semi-circle around him while he issued them with detailed instructions and, as she reached the far side of the ring, she saw Joe talking to her parents. His face looked a little pale and she wondered if his mouth was dry because he kept trying to swallow, nervously twirling his father's whip in his hand.

A moment later, a bell rang to signal that it was time for the jockeys to get on. Larry gave Joe a leg-up and then swapped places with Harry, leading Noble Warrior to give his brother a rest.

Finally, a trumpeter played a fanfare as the runners made their way on to the course. Noble Warrior didn't so much as turn a hair at this. He pricked his ears at the red buses and the fairground rides, but none of it seemed to bother him too much.

The crowd started to cheer for their preferred horse as the racecourse commentator ran through the runners and riders. Charlie puffed out her chest as he got to Number 12:

'And, riding in his very first Derby, Joe Butler takes the mount on Noble Warrior, who doesn't go anywhere without his friend Percy the pony.'

Right on cue, Percy gave a little buck and Charlie had to sit tight. The crowd clapped and whistled.

Once they'd walked in front of the grandstand for half a furlong, Larry let Noble Warrior go and it was over to Charlie to guide him down to the start. The crowds were now crammed up to the rail. She tried to keep her breathing regular as they cantered on up the hill, but she still felt a surge of adrenalin.

'Whoa, boy,' she called to Percy as they hit the top of the hill. All the other runners had pulled up to a walk for the downhill section towards the starting stalls, and Charlie pulled back to walk alongside Noble Warrior.

'He feels great,' said Joe. 'Really relaxed. All that stuff we did with music and clattering pans must've worked. Oh, and guess what I heard in the changing room? Monday Morning is supposed to be Henry Archer's best horse, which is why Bryan Dennis is riding him, but actually A Farewell to Arms has been much faster than him in the last week of training. That's why Dennis is in such a foul mood. He knows he's on the wrong one!'

'So who will you follow?' asked Charlie.

'I'll keep an eye on A Farewell to Arms, but the big dangers are Little Lion Man and Klaxon. Everyone has warned me that the French jockey Thierry Goujon, who's on Encore du Vin, is a reckless rider, so I'll steer clear of him. But I reckon I'll have to be ready for anything.'

'It's a shame. I don't think I'll see much of it because I'll be galloping across the middle, trying to get to the winning post before you do,' said Charlie.

'There'll be plenty of time to watch the replay. Don't worry about that. Just get yourself to the finish and let's see whether our aeroplane can take off!' grinned Joe, patting Noble Warrior.

They broke into a trot and jogged the last furlong to the stalls. Considering it was the biggest race in the world, Charlie was amazed how quiet it was at the start. About a hundred people in casual clothes were leaning on the rail, with a few more under the trees on the far side.

As they approached the stalls, they came closer to the other runners. Close enough for Bryan Dennis to issue one final warning. He wagged his finger at Joe as he hissed, 'Remember what I told you? This is as close as you get.'

Charlie didn't like his tone, and she didn't like him.

'Don't worry, we won't be anywhere near you,' she said, 'because, by the time we hit the straight, you'll be at the back and we'll be at the front.'

The champion jockey scowled at her.

Charlie took Percy through a gap in the rail so that she was on the inside of the track. Noble Warrior could still see them and she knew from the last week of training that, as long as he knew Percy was there at the start, he would jump out of the starting stalls and gallop forward. Then it was up to Joe to keep him with the pack until they were round Tattenham Corner and they could see Percy on the finish line.

Charlie's heart was pounding hard now. She couldn't afford to mess this up. If she didn't make it there in time and Noddy didn't win, their whole way of life would be over. The farm would have to be sold, the cows would go, and the pigs, and they might have to live in a flat that didn't allow dogs, so what would happen to Boris? She shuddered at the thought.

She had bought a racehorse by mistake; she had pushed her brothers into being part of her team; she had even made Joe spend his savings on a jockey's licence. She couldn't let them all down now.

Charlie watched Noble Warrior hesitate for a moment and then walk forward into stall 8. He was positioned in the middle to outside of the field, perfect for the first bend. He had Seamus O'Reilly's pacemaker, Harvard, one side of him and, on his outside, another O'Reilly runner called Gentle

Giant, ridden by the trainer's son, known as S. J. for Seamus Junior.

Charlie turned Percy towards the grandstand and waited for the last of the eighteen runners to be loaded into the stalls. She heard the starter calling, 'Jockeys ready?' Then there was a clunk as he released the lever.

There was a second's delay as the gates swung back before the horses reacted, and then all eighteen went from a standing start to a racing gallop. Charlie checked to see that Noble Warrior was with them – he was! – and then booted Percy in the tummy.

Crouching close to his neck like a jockey herself, together they galloped down the dusty path away from the starting stalls, past the caravans where a group was huddled round a TV.

'The gold cap, watch the gold cap!' she heard one of them say.

She caught a glimpse of her fortune-teller waving her on and shouting, 'Ride like the wind, my love! Ride like the wind!'

Charlie flashed by the fairground, past the family enclosure where picnics were scattered, past the bookies with satchels full of cash, towards the double-decker buses positioned by the finish line.

As she got closer, she could hear snatches of commentary.

'*As they come round Tattenham Corner, it's still Harvard in front, but he's beginning to tire. Journeyman is hot on his heels with Klaxon, Encore du Vin and Little Lion Man. Red Telephone Box is losing ground and struggling, Monday Morning is in mid-division with A Farewell to Arms . . .*'

Percy was straining every part of his furry little body to go as fast as he could and all that galloping downhill at home was paying dividends. Charlie hoped the same was true for Noddy.

'*. . . And angling out for a run in the middle of the course is Noble Warrior. Joe Butler coming very wide, away from the rest of the field. They've got three furlongs to run as Encore du Vin veers left towards the rail, hampering Little Lion Man and A Farewell to Arms who was trying to make ground . . .*'

Ahead of her, Charlie could see the gap in the rails by the finish line, but she didn't recognize the security guard. Surely they hadn't changed shifts already?

Percy skidded to a halt.

'Please, you have to let us through!' Charlie panted.

'I most certainly will not,' said the new guard. 'The Derby is underway.'

'Dave, Dave!' cried a voice behind him. 'It's fine – she's got special permission. She's the trainer of the horse who's going to win.'

Her friendly security guard waved a betting ticket at his colleague and let Charlie through the gap on to the course. Just in time.

Charlie could see Joe's gold cap wide of the main pack, but Noble Warrior didn't seem to be accelerating. He was going well enough to be level with the main group, but he wasn't finishing the race as fast as she knew he could. There were so many distractions, so much going on, that Charlie wondered if Noble Warrior couldn't see them at the winning post.

Luckily, Percy came to the rescue. He let out a loud whinny and Charlie saw Noble Warrior's ears prick.

The response was immediate.

'... *It's Journeyman and Little Lion Man pulling clear. Freddie Mould and Fingal O'Connor in a real tussle, but here comes Noble Warrior. Wide and late and very, very fast, Noble Warrior is gaining ground with every stride. Half a furlong to run and he might just get there ...*'

As the horses thundered towards them, Charlie heard Joe shouting at her. She couldn't make out what he was saying, but it sounded like, 'Go away!'

Of course! She was only a few metres past the winning post. She needed to be much further beyond it, or Noble Warrior would slow down on the line, rather than racing through it. She swung Percy round and galloped away.

'... *Noble Warrior still closing, Noble Warrior is getting there, but is it too late?*' The commentator was screaming and the whole crowd seemed to be shouting with him.

'... *It's Little Lion Man, Journeyman and Noble Warrior as they hit the line. Impossible to split them. What a finish to this year's Derby!*'

'PHOTOGRAPH, PHOTOGRAPH!' said the announcer.

As Percy finally ran out of puff, Noble Warrior cantered up to him, heaving with effort. Even Joe was out of breath.

'That,' he panted, 'was . . . incredible.'

They slowed down to a walk and turned back towards the grandstand.

Charlie hardly dared ask. 'Did you win?'

Joe pulled down his goggles and shook his head.

'I don't know. But win, lose or draw, this is the best racehorse in the country and you are the only trainer who could make him show it.'

He dropped the reins and flopped forward on to Noddy's neck, throwing his arms round it and hugging him tight. When he sat back up, Charlie saw that he was crying. He held his whip up to his mouth and kissed it.

'My dad always wanted me to ride in the Derby and I just wish that he could be here to see it,' he said.

Fingal O'Connor trotted past on Little Lion Man.

'Well done!' he shouted. 'I think you got it.'

Charlie looked up to see Harry and Larry running down the track towards them, their parents not far behind.

'What a run!' exclaimed Harry as he put the leading rein through Noble Warrior's bridle and patted his neck. 'Good boy!'

Larry ran towards Charlie.

'I was watching you while Harry followed the race. You went so fast, it was incredible! I couldn't believe you could stay on when you were coming down that hill, but you did. I don't think anyone with skinny legs could've done it.'

Charlie looked at her brother to check he wasn't teasing her. He was grinning and patting her leg. 'These might just have won us the Derby.'

'My thunder thighs, you mean?' said Charlie.

'No. Your powerful legs,' replied Larry.

A three-note alarm came through the loudspeakers.

'Here is the result of the photograph,' said the announcer. 'In first place, Number 12, Noble Warrior, owned by the Bass family, trained by Charlotte Bass and ridden by Joe Butler. Second is Number 8, Little Lion Man, owned by the Big Three Syndicate, trained by Seamus O'Reilly and ridden by Fingal O'Connor. And third is Number 6, Journeyman, owned by His Highness Prince Abdul, trained by Sir Malcolm Buckwell and ridden by Freddie Mould. The distances were a nose and a short head. A nose and a short head.'

Joe raised his whip into the air and looked to the heavens.

'WE DID IT!'

The whole family screamed with excitement.

'No wonder it took them so long to work it out,' said Mrs Bass. 'That's the closest finish in Derby history.'

'Will we be safe now?' Charlie asked. 'I mean the farm. Will we be able to keep the farm?'

'Keep it?' said Mrs Bass. 'We can more than keep it. We can pay off the mortgage and resurface the drive, mend the roof and get new chairs for the kitchen. You, Charlie Bass, are a miracle worker!'

As they walked back down the track, Charlie tried to take it all in. She looked up at the big screen to see the replay of the finish and there was Joe, a flash of green and gold, coming down the middle of the track when everyone else was bumping into each other on the inside rail.

She was thrilled that they had won the Derby, the most historic race in the world, but more than that she was just so relieved that the cows and the pigs and the chickens and Boris the Border terrier would be able to stay with them and they could keep living the life they loved. For some people, winning the Derby could change everything, but Charlie had wanted to win it to keep everything the same.

As they walked past the placed horses, Seamus O'Reilly ran towards her and held out his hand.

'I want to shake the hand of the Derby-winning trainer. You did an amazing job with that horse. I know at least two other trainers who had given up on him. Well done to you. And to you, Joe. Any time you want to ride for me, you'd be more than welcome.'

Charlie was amazed he could be so sporting in defeat, but Seamus seemed genuinely happy for them.

The commentator was back on the PA system, having taken a swig of water to help him recover his voice.

'Ladies and gentlemen, your applause, please, for the Derby winner, NOBLE WARRIOR!'

Charlie kicked Percy into a trot so that he could get in front of Noddy and guide him down in front of the grandstand. The crowd roared their approval.

She heard barking from the inside of the course and, right by the gap where she had come through, she saw Alex and Jasmine Williams with Polly. In Polly's arms was Boris.

'We had to bring him! We couldn't miss a day like this!' shouted Polly.

'Are you friends of the trainer?' asked Charlie's friendly security guard.

'I'm her *best* friend,' said Polly. 'And this is her dog.'

'Well, in that case, I must let you through and, if you could say thank you to the young lady from me, I'd be most grateful. She told me to put a bet on Noble Warrior and I did. She's just won me ten thousand pounds!'

As they turned into the tiny circle of the winner's enclosure, now packed with photographers and TV cameras, Charlie looked up to the Royal Box to see if the Queen was watching and saw a familiar purple hat leaning over the balcony to get a better view.

'Just the winner, please,' said the bowler-hatted man in charge of the winner's enclosure, waving at Charlie to hold Percy back.

'But we have to be inside too,' said Charlie.

'I know, I know,' he said. 'Everyone wants to come in, but it's only the winner who's allowed.'

Charlie didn't want to start an argument so she waited.

Harry tried to lead Noble Warrior forward, but at the mouth of the winner's enclosure he froze. He wouldn't budge an inch.

'Honestly, sir, he won't move without the pony,' Joe explained to the man in the bowler hat. 'We won't get him in there at all unless you let Percy in first.'

'Fine,' sighed the bowler-hatted man. 'In you go.'

As Charlie walked into the winner's circle, followed by Joe on Noble Warrior, the commentator said, 'Your Majesty, my lords, ladies and gentlemen, please welcome the longest-priced ever winner of the Derby, who has run the fastest time recorded for the mile and a half here at Epsom – Noble Warrior, owned by the Bass family, trained by Charlotte Bass, ridden by Joe Butler and ably assisted by Percy the Pony.'

On hearing his name, Percy put one leg forward, bent the other and bowed his head. Charlie leaned back to make sure she didn't tumble over his neck, and waved to the crowd. They cheered so loudly she thought the grandstand might fall down. Joe touched the peak of his cap and slid down off Noble Warrior's back.

Immediately, a group of men surrounded him to pat his back and hug him.

'Well done, lad! Your dad would be proud,' Charlie heard one of them say.

Joe's eyes were red again as he came towards her, but he was smiling and she could tell they were tears of joy.

'My dad's mates from Newmarket,' he said. 'I'd no idea they were coming.'

'Look who else is here,' said Charlie, pointing to the back of the winner's enclosure where Polly was holding Boris tight.

All the photographers were clamouring for a shot, so Joe went to stand one side of Noble Warrior while Harry held him on the other. It was a lovely gathering, but one person wasn't happy. Flattening his ears, Percy started to squeal with anger.

'I'm so sorry!' cried Charlie. 'He's upset at the lack of attention. If you let us stand next to Noble Warrior too, he'll be fine.'

Suddenly the photographers were pushed to one side by a group of muscular security guards. A whisper ran through the crowd and Charlie looked round to see what was happening. She saw Polly pointing back to the tunnel next to the weighing room. As she raised her arm, Boris jumped down and headed for Charlie.

In the kerfuffle, Charlie saw Polly mouthing something.

'The screen. Look at the screen!' she seemed to be saying.

Only it wasn't 'the screen'.

Charlie turned back to see the Queen standing right in front of her.

'Many congratulations to you all,' said the Queen. 'I wanted to come down to see the pony for myself. And Noble Warrior, of course.'

Her Majesty's white-gloved hand reached forward to stroke Noble Warrior on the nose. He lowered his head and accepted it politely.

Even Harry and Larry were lost for words.

'Thank you, Your Majesty,' said Joe, speaking for all of them.

'I really couldn't be more pleased,' the Queen continued. 'And not just because I got Noble Warrior in the sweepstake. I love good horsemanship and I've seen more evidence of that today than in many a year. Now, do come up to the Royal Box for tea, please. I want to hear all about your farm and, of course, about Percy.'

She turned to stroke Percy, who flattened his ears and bared his teeth. Quick as a flash, Mr Bass put his own hand in the way and was rewarded with a pair of teeth clamped on to his arm.

'We'd love to have tea,' he said through the pain. 'But I'm afraid we've got to get back home. Princess Anne gets very grumpy if she's not fed on time.'

'So I've heard,' said the Queen with a smile.

'I think we can help out there, Bill,' said Alex Williams. 'I'll ring the yard and send over a couple of my staff to do the milking and feeding.'

'Yes, let us sort it out,' said Mrs Williams. 'You don't win the Derby every day and, for pity's sake, it's tea with the Queen!'

'Give us half an hour to sort the horses out and we'd love to accept,' said Charlie. Then, suddenly remembering her manners, 'I mean, we'd love to accept, *Your Majesty*.'

Epilogue

Next day, the front pages could talk of nothing else.

FARMING FAMILY MILK THE DERBY! said the headline in the *Moon*.

OUTSIDER WINS THE DERBY IN RECORD TIME! wrote the *Racing Post*.

SCHOOLGIRL FINDS THE KEY TO THE RACEHORSE WHO WOULDN'T GALLOP! announced the *Siren*.

DONKEY WINS THE DERBY! screamed the *Messenger*.

At breakfast, Harry and Larry were fighting over the newspapers while Mrs Bass was emailing the bank to explain what had happened and that they would very soon be paying back all the money that was due. Mr Bass had milked the cows and was watching the replay of the Derby for the third time.

Joe and Charlie had slipped away to take Noble Warrior and Percy for a gentle walk to the river. They stood the horses in the ice-cold water for half an hour, and sat comfortably in silence, each lost in their own thoughts, while Boris dug holes on the bank, looking up occasionally to check Charlie was still there.

Finally, Joe smiled.

'Bryan Dennis said "Well done" to me in the changing room. He didn't smile or anything like that, but still . . .'

'Gosh!' said Charlie. 'Maybe he's not all bad after all. He must've felt a bit stupid, though. He finished last in the end, didn't he?'

'Yeah.'

'The Queen asked me whether I was planning to train any more horses,' said Charlie. 'She said she's got a few tricky ones that might like being here on the farm.'

'What did you say?' asked Joe.

'I said I might have to wait until I finish school.'

'Fair enough,' laughed Joe. 'I don't suppose many trainers have maths lessons to worry about! Did you hear what Seamus O'Reilly said to me about riding for him? Would you mind?'

Charlie looked him straight in the eye.

'Would I mind? I'd mind, Joe Butler, if you didn't. You've just won the Derby and you should ride for anyone and everyone who wants you. Just as long as you can still find time for Noddy too.'

'I won't miss anything with Noble Warrior. We've got more races to win before this season is out. There's the Eclipse, the King George, the Arc, even the Breeder's Cup in America. He could win them all.'

'Did you see Prince Abdul, who owns Journeyman?' said Charlie. 'He stopped me as we were taking Noddy back to the stables and offered two million pounds for him.'

Joe sucked air through his teeth.

'Two million?'

'Yup. I didn't bother checking with Mum or Dad, but I told him he wasn't for sale. Anyway, if he wanted to buy Noddy, he'd have to buy Percy as well and he'd cost at least four million.'

They both laughed at the idea of the palomino pony costing twice as much as a racehorse who had just won the Derby.

'Someone might even pay that, though,' said Joe. 'Noddy's that good.'

'They can offer anything they want,' said Charlie firmly. 'They aren't for sale. Not today, not tomorrow, not ever.'

As she spoke, Percy put his nose in the water and started pawing with his near foreleg. Water splashed everywhere. And, keeping perfect time, Percy played a tune from his bottom that sounded like a trumpet salute.

'Mind you,' laughed Charlie, ducking away, 'I might regret that decision.'

Listen!

It's
THE RACEHORSE WHO WOULDN'T GALLOP
on audiobook!

Now you can hear Clare Balding bring the characters to life in her own words.

Scan the QR code to listen to an extract.

po.st/RacehorseExtract

Author Q & A

Puffin met up with author Clare Balding to ask her some nosy questions. Here's what she had to say . . .

Q. Why did you decide to write about horses?

A. I grew up surrounded by horses (my father was a racehorse trainer) so it seemed a good idea to stick to something I knew well! Also I love horses and I think they can bring out the best in us as human beings.

Q. Were you like Charlie when you were growing up?

A. I was much naughtier, but I can certainly identify with being the outsider at school and with having 'powerful legs'! Also I loved trying to coax difficult ponies or horses to better behaviour and to try to help them fulfil their potential.

Q. Did you base Harry and Larry on people you know? They seem pretty awful!

A. I have two nephews and a niece whose age gaps are similar but Jonno and Toby aren't nearly as badly behaved as Harry and Larry, although they find them very funny characters. Flora, who is five, was the inspiration for Charlie.

. You've written books for adults before, but this is our first book for children. Was it easy to write this book, or hard?

. The story was in my head, but making sure the plot worked, eveloping the characters and keeping it moving all took a t of work. I rewrote nearly all of it and took out or added ctions as I went along. Writing fiction is fun, but it is a allenge!

. How long does it take to write a book?

. It does depend on how easily the creative juices are flowing d some chapters or episodes (such as the fortune-teller scene Epsom) come really naturally and fast. The hardest part is arting and I find the first chapter the most difficult. I then try give myself a month of regular writing (every day if possible) get the bulk of the plot and characterization worked out.

. Is it really possible to ride a cow, like Charlie does?

. Yes, but it wouldn't be very comfortable and they wouldn't able to carry heavy weights as horses do. I based that on at the former champion jockey Kieren Fallon told me. didn't ride a horse until he was eighteen, but he jumped plenty of cows when he was young.

Q. What would be your one piece of advice for someone just starting out who wants to ride or train professionally?

A. Go to a trainer in your school holidays and definitely go to the British Racing School (as Joe does in the book). My father and my brother have had many young boys and girls at their stables who have never ridden before and end up riding in races. One of them even won the Derby.

Q. What is your favourite racecourse and why?

A. I love Ascot for its size and grandeur and I enjoy Goodwood for its landscape and relative intimacy, but for jump racing nothing beats Cheltenham!

Q. Will you be writing more books? If so, what will they be about?

A. Definitely. I will see what adventures Charlie might have next as I think her patience with animals and her problem-solving skills could be useful in other arenas.

Q. You present on so many different sports all around the world. Do you have a favourite place and a favourite sporting event?

A. London 2012 was the ultimate highlight and to work on the Olympics and Paralympics in my home city will never be topped. I love the big multi-sport events and have enjoyed various Winter Olympics and Commonwealth Games as well, but of course I love anything with horses – racing, eventing, show jumping and dressage are all wonderful to cover.

Thanks for answering our questions, Clare!

Pony Grooming – Top Tips!

Here are some inside tips to get your pony (or horse!) looking fit for a meeting with the Queen!

Treat the feet!

Take a good look at your pony's hooves when you pick them out. Does he need a supplement to help with horn growth? Could he benefit from some luxurious hoof grease? Give your pony's hooves a good wash so you can really see what you've got down there, then treat the feet!

Marvellous manes

Give manes some TLC. Use a detangling spray to make manes more manageable, and then transform your pony's mop into his crowning glory by using a gorgeous conditioner or mane shine! Keep manes looking good by only ever using your fingers or a body brush – never a plastic curry comb, which splits the hair!

Head to tail

A face brush works well on your pony's head – or, even better, rinse an old towel in some hot water, wring it out and give your pony a hot-towel face wash! Ponies love it and it brings up the shine!

Body beautiful

A rubber curry comb, used in a circular motion, is fantastic at bringing up all the dead hair out of the coat. Once you've been all over your pony in this way, brush with your body brush and then try the hot towel treatment, as described for his face, all over to get rid of any leftover dust and grease. Do this every day for a week and you'll really see a transformation. A spray conditioner can then do its job!

The tail-end

Detangle the clean tail with a spray, brush with a body brush and use conditioner to make it look gorgeous.

Bath time

Wait for a warm, sunny day then use a proper horse shampoo, rinse him well afterwards and make sure he doesn't get cold as he dries off.

Insider top tip!

If your pony gets dusty, simply dunk your metal curry comb in a bucket of warm water, shake off and run your body brush over it before using on your pony. Repeat this every four or five strokes, and you'll see the dust disappear. This is great for ponies growing out their clip – try it and see!

Tools of the trade!

Body brush – removes grease from the coat – use with hot water to get rid of dust

Hoof pick – lets you see the condition of the hooves

Dandy brush – removes dried mud from ponies and dead hair from the inside of rugs!

Face brush – soft brush for use on the face

Rubber curry comb – perfect for getting rid of your pony's old, dead winter coat

Sweat scraper – to remove water after a bath

Metal curry comb – used to clean the body brush – NOT for use on your pony!

Plastic curry comb – removes mud and moulting hair

Flick brush – flicks dirt off your pony

Fantastic Facts!

Read these facts about ponies and horses. How many did you already know?

- There are more than two hundred breeds of ponies, but the Shetland Pony is the best-known.

- When compared to standard-sized horses, ponies are actually stronger, pound for pound.

- During the Industrial Revolution, some ponies were called 'pit ponies' as they were used to haul coal.

- Ponies and horses have two blind spots where they cannot see. One blind spot is behind them and if they sense some-one or something behind them, they will give a powerful kick.

- In the wild, ponies often live in harsh, bleak areas such as moors and fields, where they are able to survive with little food.

- All members of the horse family have just one toe (a hoof) on each foot. For this reason they are often called 'odd-toed animals'.

- Stallions (male horses) defend their territory and protect their mares (female horses) by lashing out with their front feet.

Horses have the largest eyes of any land mammal.

A baby horse of one year or younger is called a foal.

Horse-riding is often used as a form of therapy for people with disabilities.

Horses can sleep both lying down and standing up.

Horses usually gallop at around 27 mph but the fastest recorded sprinting speed of a horse was 55 mph!

Estimates suggest that there are around 60 million horses in the world.

About an hour after a foal is born, it can stand up, and within a few hours it is able to trot along by its mother.

The scientific name for a horse is *Equus ferus caballus*.

Horses have excellent senses, including good hearing, eyesight and a tremendous sense of balance.

Quiz!

How closely were you paying attention when you were reading this book? Take our quiz to find out! But beware – the questions start off easy but get quite tricky at the end!

> **Tip!** Write your answers in pencil so the pen doesn't show through the page!

Q1. What is Charlie's surname?

....

Q2. How old is Charlie?

....

Q3. What is the name of Charlie's cheeky pony?

....

Q4. What nickname is given to Noble Warrior?

....

Q5. What are the names of Charlie's brothers?

....

Q6. Without looking at the front of the book, who illustrated *The Racehorse Who Wouldn't Gallop*?

....

Q7. Who buys Noble Warrior and Percy at the 'Horses in Training' sale?

....

8. What is the name of Charlie's family dog?

....

9. Which celebrity does Charlie meet after the Derby race?

....

10. What is unusual about Percy the pony's eyes?

....

11. What unkind nickname do Charlie's brothers call her?

....

12. Who does Charlie meet at the fairground just before the Derby?

....

13. And how much does she try to charge Charlie for her services?

....

14. Which colour jacket does Joe wear to race Noble Warrior?

....

15. What is the name of Charlie's family farm?

....

16. What is the name of the newspaper that prints the awful story
about Charlie's dad?

....

17. At which racecourse is the Derby held?

....

18. Name one of the cows at Charlie's farm.

....

19. What is the name of the posh riding stables near Charlie's farm?

....

20. What number does Noble Warrior have in the Derby?

....

Now turn over the page to see how many you got right!

The Racehorse Who Wouldn't Gallop – Answers!

Check your answers to the quiz below. How did you do?

1. Bass
2. Ten years old
3. Percy
4. Noddy
5. Harry and Larry
6. Tony Ross
7. Charlie
8. Boris
9. The Queen
10. One is blue and one is brown

11. 'Thunder Thighs'
12. A fortune-teller
13. Twenty pounds
14. Green and gold
15. Folly Farm
16. The *Moon*
17. Epsom
18. Princess Anne
    Windy Bottom
    Creamy
    Hermione Granger
    Madonna
    Jane Eyre
    Moll Flanders
19. Cherrydown Stables
20. Number 12

15–20 correct:	Astounding! You are a true champion – first place!
10–14 correct:	Well done! You were just pipped to the post, but you're still in second place!
5–9 correct:	Not too bad. It's a third place rosette for you – better luck next time!
1–4 correct:	Oh dear. You may need to go back and read the story again to brush up on your know-how!

17

WAYS TO
BOND WITH YOUR
FAVE PONY

Check out these 17 ways to strengthen your bond with your fave pony. You'll be best friends in no time!

1 Give him a good groom and find all his fave itchy spots. Most ponies love a scratch at the base of their neck or behind their ears!

2 Take him for a walk and let him find the best grazing spot for a snack.

3 Talk to him! He might not understand exactly what you're saying, but ponies can understand your tone of voice.

4 Take a break from the arena and go for a nice hack – your fave pony will love going for an adventure!

5 Pamper your pony by practising plaiting his mane. He'll love all the extra fuss.

6 Cut up some apples and carrots and hide them in his haynet. He'll have a great time finding them all!

7 Hang out with him in the field. Ponies are at their happiest when turned out, and sitting and watching your fave pony enjoy the sunshine is a great bonding experience.

8 If it's a really hot day, why not give him a bath? It'll help to keep him nice and cool, and he'll look fab afterwards – bonus!

9 Play some gymkhana games with your friends at the yard. Doing fun activities with your fave pony will mean you'll be best friends in no time!

10 Find out what his fave treat is. Apples and mints are a safe bet, but some ponies have more exotic tastes and like treats such as bananas and pears!

11 Learn to spot basic health problems in your fave pony. Being able to tell when he's uncomfortable and helping to make him happy again will make you his friend for life.

12 Set up an unmounted obstacle course at the yard and practise guiding him through it.

13 Give his tack a really good clean. That way it'll be comfortable for him when you ride.

14 Remember to tell him when he's done something good. A well-timed pat will make him want to do well again.

15 Make sure he has a cosy bed. Skip out any droppings or wet patches and fluff up his bedding so it's really comfy.

16 Visit him even on days when you won't be riding – that way, he won't associate you with work.

17 Give him a big kiss and tell him how fab he is!

Design your silks!

If you were going to race in the Derby, what would your riding silks look like? Colour in some ideas here and remember to make them super-colourful to stand out in the dash for the winning post!

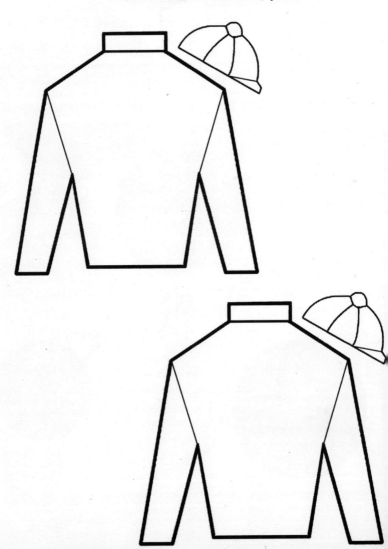